"Melody does it again. She reaches inside a hurting girl and gives her story a voice, writing it in a way so compelling that putting this book down is nearly impossible. Girls who have experienced this horrible thing will find someone who understands, and those who have not may find understanding of those who have as well as a reason to be watchful in relationships that seem so wonderful."

—LISSA HALLS JOHNSON, author of nineteen books, including *Kirk Cameron: Still Growing*

DAMAGED

A VIOLATED TRUST

Melody Carlson

NAVPRESS
Discipleship Inside Out

THINK

Discipleship Inside Out™

NavPress is the publishing ministry of The Navigators, an international Christian organization and leader in personal spiritual development. NavPress is committed to helping people grow spiritually and enjoy lives of meaning and hope through personal and group resources that are biblically rooted, culturally relevant, and highly practical.

For a free catalog go to www.NavPress.com
or call 1.800.366.7788 in the United States or 1.800.839.4769 in Canada.

© 2011 by Melody Carlson

NAVPRESS, the NAVPRESS logo, TH1NK, and the TH1NK logo are registered trademarks of NavPress. Absence of ® in connection with marks of NavPress or other parties does not indicate an absence of registration of those marks.

ISBN-13: 978-1-60006-950-5

Cover design by Faceout Studio, Charles Brock
Cover image by istockphoto.com

Published in association with the literary agency of Sara A. Fortenberry

Some of the anecdotal illustrations in this book are true to life and are included with the permission of the persons involved. All other illustrations are composites of real situations, and any resemblance to people living or dead is coincidental.

Carlson, Melody.
  Damaged : a violated trust / Melody Carlson.
    p. cm.
  ISBN 978-1-60006-950-5
  I. Title.
  PZ7.C216637Dam 2011
  [Fic]—dc23

                            2011020793

Printed in the United States of America

1 2 3 4 5 6 7 8 / 15 14 13 12 11

Other Novels by Melody Carlson

To be fair, it's not completely my mom's fault that I'm moving out today. In some ways it feels like I've just outgrown her and it's time to take a new path. Even so, as I shove my last load into the back of Dad's SUV, balancing my guitar case on top of a confused heap of all my worldly goods, I feel guilty.

"Ready to go, kiddo?" Dad closes the back door and smiles hopefully.

I know he's desperate to get out of here. He's already attempted an exchange of words with my older brother, Sean. As I anticipated, it went badly and I can tell Dad's eager to put as much distance as possible between himself and this place. It's the same house he and Mom bought more than twenty years ago, and now he hates it like poison. Divorce is just like that.

"I, uh, I think I should do one last check inside," I tell him.

He glances at his watch. "Well, make it snappy, *okay*? I have a racquetball game scheduled for tonight, and if we get out of here in the next few minutes, I think I can still make it."

I nod and hurry back into the house, where my mom is anchored to the same spot on the couch where she's been sulking all morning. Still wearing her faded pink bathrobe and bed-head hair that's even more dulled with streaks of gray, she looks like she's about to cry again. She also looks a lot older than forty-two, not to mention a lot older than my dad. I'm sure she would lay the blame for her premature aging at my feet . . . or Dad's.

I desperately want to say something to her, something that will make this all okay. But I don't have those magic words, so I hurry past the living room, down the hallway, and back to my old bedroom, where I just stand looking around the cleared-out space.

My room, my private getaway for my entire life of sixteen years, has never looked so tidy . . . or so barren. But despite being stripped down to its scarred-up periwinkle walls, naked mattress, empty closet, and beat-up pine dresser, this space still feels weirdly familiar and strangely comforting. And for a brief moment I wonder if I need to rethink my decision to leave. Is this a mistake?

"Did you forget something, Haley?"

I turn to see my mom's tired brown eyes peering curiously at me. Again, I wish I could invent the right words to say . . . something to make our parting less painful. Then Mom holds up my old Bible. At least I assume it's my Bible. I haven't seen it for a while.

"Or maybe you *meant* to leave this behind?" She waves the light blue book in my face like she's turning in state's evidence.

I won't admit it, but the truth is I *did* mean to leave my Bible behind. But I just shrug, take the book from her, and tuck it under my arm.

"I found it in the drawer of the *coffee table*." The way she proclaims this feels like an insinuation, like I purposely hid it there.

"I know this is hard for you, Mom." My voice is tight. The words are sticking together like a big wad of gum. "I . . . I'm sorry."

"Don't worry about me, Haley. I'll be just fine. You're the one who's making a very big mistake." She folds her arms across her front and frowns. She's scowled so much lately that the expression will probably carve itself permanently into her face. Not that she cares much about her appearance. That's obvious by the way she dressed to see my dad this morning — not. According to Mom, vanity is the Devil's device.

"I just can't do this anymore. It's too hard." More than anything, I wish I hadn't come back into the house, hadn't tried to patch this up. How many times have I been down this road with her? I should know each step by heart. I do know this: It's a dead end.

"Then you should run away. Just like your father did. But don't forget, even if you can run from me, you can't run from God. He will eventually catch you — what he'll do with you when he does . . ." She sighs and actually wrings her hands. "Well, it won't be my responsibility."

"I'm sorry this is hurting you," I quietly tell her. "I hope you know I still love you."

"I love you too, Haley. But you're *still* making a big mistake. Your father has turned his back on God. If you go live with him, you'll do the same."

"How can you know that?"

"I *know*." Her voice is getting stronger now, like she's about to launch into another one of her sermons.

I make a move toward the door but she blocks me.

"Just because you don't like my rules doesn't mean they weren't in your best interests. 'A fool despises discipline, but a wise man welcomes a rebuke.'"

"I know, I know." I hold up my hands. "I've heard all this before, Mom."

"You might hear with your ears, but your heart has gone deaf."

Okay, I realize my mistake. It's useless trying to reason with a crazy woman. It's like she thinks she's God's ordained prophetess, spewing her warnings and condemnations to anyone stupid enough to cross her path or listen. I am so tired of it. In fact, I have decided if that's what God is really like — cold and judgmental and mean — then I guess Mom is right. I probably will turn my back on him.

"I have to go," I say in a controlled tone. "Dad is waiting."

"Oh yes, don't keep the lying betrayer waiting. We wouldn't want to inconvenience that loathsome sinner, now would we?"

I know her words are the result of a lot of pain, and part of me wants to hug her one last time, but she looks so angry, as if she's wrapped in a barbed-wire fence with a big Keep Out sign. "I love you, Mom, but I gotta go."

She steps aside but her expression is even frostier. "Just because the judge let you decide where to live doesn't mean it's the right decision, Haley. Man's laws and God's laws are not equal. Someday you will understand what a mistake you've made. But remember this — do not expect me to come rescue you when you fall flat on your face."

"I won't." I push past her, holding my tongue and knowing that nothing I can say will make any difference. Sometimes I truly think my mom is losing her sanity. To me the saying of "being so heavenly minded you're no earthly good" is an understatement when it comes to my mom. I even said this to her once, but she simply launched into a sermon about how this earth was going to burn since it was all evil anyway. Whatever.

I'm almost out the door when Sean stops me. "Take care, sis," he mumbles, giving me a squeeze on the shoulder. For him, that's quite demonstrative.

"You take care too." I give him another hug, but just like with the last one, when I said good-bye earlier, Sean doesn't respond. He just stands there hard and cold, like a big boulder or a marble statue of my brother. I can almost imagine he's still in his army uniform, except that back then, back before he left for the Middle East, his smile was genuine and his hug was like a big friendly teddy bear. He didn't get injured in Iraq, not so you can see, but he is like the walking wounded now. He's definitely not the same Sean McLean who marched off to war, and I don't know if my other brother will ever come home. I look into his sad blue eyes. "If Mom gets to you," I whisper, "you could always come out and live with Dad and me in California."

He just shakes his head. "Mom needs me."

"Yes." I pat him on the back. "Maybe you can help her." I tell him good-bye for the second time, then, blinking back tears, I jog out to the SUV, slide into the passenger seat, and let out a huge sigh.

"Find what you were looking for?" Dad's already starting the engine.

I toss my well-worn Bible into the backseat and shrug, trying not to give in to crying like a baby. The whole point of doing this is to show Dad and the rest of the world that I am mature, nearly grown up. It won't look good to break down and cry.

"They're going to be okay, Haley."

I turn and stare at him. "What makes you so sure?"

"Oh, you know what they say, baby doll. Time heals all wounds." He grins. "Or wounds all heels."

"Mostly . . . I worry about Sean."

He nods. "So do I."

"Mom's always telling him to just pray his way through everything."

Dad shakes his head, but I can see his jaw tightening.

"I think Sean might be able to get some help," I go on. "I mean at the VA hospital. I read online that they're doing some counseling and psychological evaluations and stuff. But when I told him about it, he said he didn't need any help."

"Maybe he's not ready."

"But he's so miserable, Dad."

"I know. But sometimes people have to hit rock bottom before they look up and reach for help."

"Has that ever happened to you? I mean *rock bottom*."

Dad drums his fingers on the steering wheel with a thoughtful expression as he waits for the light to change. "I'm not really sure. I mean, I felt pretty low when I left your mom — that was rough and it might've been my rock bottom — but then I kind of bounced back too. But you know me, Haley, the perennial optimist." He grins again, and I'm suddenly reminded of better times and how when my dad smiled it always seemed like the sun came out.

"I think some optimism might be nice for a change." I return his smile and start to relax inside.

"So, how about some music? We've got a long drive ahead, and I'm going to need something to keep me awake after getting up at two in the morning to come pick you up."

"Music is good."

So Dad turns on his stereo, and while he rocks out to some old fogy tunes, I ponder over what I'm getting myself into. I've only been to my dad's place twice. Once for Christmas and once for a couple of weeks the summer before last. But back then I never imagined that life with Mom would get so bad I'd actually choose my dad over her. I find it hard to believe that only three years ago, I was solidly on Mom's side. So much so that it was difficult to visit my dad—since he was the traitor who'd run out on us.

My parents split up shortly after my mom began going to a different church. I realize now that their marriage had already been in trouble, and she was looking for some answers. At first I thought this new church was just what she needed. Especially after the divorce. Her ladies' Bible study group became her safety net. It even seemed to shake her out of her funk and bring her to life. And at first I didn't mind going to church with her. It was definitely different from what I'd been used to, but I figured if it helped Mom, why not?

But after a year of this new church, Mom started going off the deep end. It was about this same time that I started to question things, and as a result Mom and I started to argue. It didn't help matters when I quit going to church with her. But what was I supposed to do, check my brain at the door? The pastor acted like everyone should just believe everything he said—like he was God's gift to these poor lost sheep. And I have to say that a lot of the stuff he said was pretty weird.

It didn't take long until Mom started to sound just like the pastor. She was talking differently, thinking differently, acting differently. Almost like she'd been brainwashed. Anyway, I got the distinct impression I was losing her.

On my fifteenth birthday, she surprised me—not by making a cake, not by getting me a present or even a card, but instead by hitting me with this: "God told me you are not to date until you turn eighteen, Haley Michelle."

Too shocked to respond, I just chalked it up to one more weird and fundamentalist thing she'd learned from her women's group. I hoped it was only a phase, something she'd get over by the time a real opportunity to date occurred. But the no-dating rule only seemed to snowball. Not only was I not allowed to date until I was of voting age, I was not allowed to go to dances or other social gatherings where boys were present. Naturally that covered almost everything at my high school.

Even though I rarely even had a conversation with a guy, I was lectured regularly on the evils of boys in general and was spied on more times than I can remember. It came to a head at the end of last school year.

It was one of those delicious spring days, and I actually felt like a normal girl for a nice change. Bryce Thurston (my first and only boyfriend) was walking me home from school, and we were laughing and joking and holding hands—acting like what I assume normal teens are supposed to act like. And it was so fun!

Of course, I had no idea my mom was hiding behind the Schulers' hedge as Bryce and I passed by. Seriously, whose mom does that? I nearly had a heart attack when she leaped out from the shadows.

"What do you think you are doing?" she demanded, shaking her finger at me.

After recovering from the shock, I went into embarrassment mode when I noticed she was wearing an ugly old Christmas sweater and matted pink fuzzy slippers. Naturally, Bryce excused himself and took off in the opposite direction.

That was the day Mom decided she would find a way to afford the tuition at her church's private academy—a pathetic little school with about twenty unfortunate kids between the ages of five and eighteen.

A few days later, I did some online legal research and discovered that at sixteen, I was old enough to petition a judge for the right to live with my other parent. And that's exactly what I did. Much to my mom's displeasure, after I presented my case, the judge ruled in my favor. It helped that my grades were high and I'd never been in any kind of trouble. I even presented some letters from my teachers and school counselor. Also, the judge seemed familiar with Mom's church and she didn't agree with forcing one's religion onto one's young adult children. But it's a bittersweet victory.

As we get closer to the California border, I feel myself drifting off to the sound of my dad's favorite band, the Eagles, playing "Hotel California." "Such a lovely place . . . such a lovely face . . ." I imagine those lyrics are for me and hope I will be welcome here "any time of year."

CHAPTER 2

"Here we are," Dad says as he pulls into his space in the condominium parking lot. "Home sweet home."

I hear the sarcasm in his voice, but I don't really care. I'm just glad to get out of the car and stretch my legs. I'm surprised at how warm the air feels, especially for October. But then I'm not in Oregon anymore. Dad's condominium is about thirty minutes from Fresno, where he works for a big insurance company. And while it's not really Southern California, it feels like a different world to me. Instead of evergreen trees, there are palms, and the air feels dryer too.

"Is the swimming pool still open?" I ask.

"Oh, sure." He opens the back of his SUV.

"Looks like not much has changed around here." I reach for my guitar case and another bag.

"Nah, but sometimes that's a good thing." He grabs a plastic crate and a duffle bag. "Let's get this stuff unloaded ASAP, okay?"

"No problem." I follow him as he practically sprints with his arms full, bounding up the stairs to his third-floor unit. I'm still caught off guard by how much younger he seems than when he was living at home. He seems so much younger than Mom, even though he's three years older. Maybe some people just age differently. Hopefully I'll take after my dad.

It takes about an hour, but we get everything unloaded in time for Dad to make his racquetball date. "You're sure you don't mind me taking off like this?" He slings a strap of his gym bag over his shoulder.

"No, Dad, I'm fine. Remember our agreement: You're going to treat me like an adult and I'm going to act like one."

He grins and grabs a ball cap off the coatrack. "There's not much in the fridge, but help yourself to anything. Or if you want to wait, we can run out and grab a bite to eat when I get back."

"Sounds good."

After he leaves, I lock the front door. It's not that I'm scared exactly, but I'm just cautious. We lived in a pretty small town in southern Oregon, but my mom always insisted on locking and dead bolting the doors, whether we were home or out, and I guess old habits die hard. I check my pocket for the key Dad gave me, worried I might've lost it already like I did last time I was here, but thankfully it's still there.

Now I take a quick tour of Dad's condo, which looks almost exactly like it did before. Same black leather sofa and easy chair (Dad's attempt at a bachelor pad). Same metal and glass-topped tables and same big-screen TV that I was so impressed with. Same fake ficus plant (probably the same dust, too). It's in a gigantic pot wedged into a corner by the sliding doors that lead to the terrace and overlook the pool. I'll admit the pool looks pretty good—a bright turquoise spot surrounded by hot-looking terra-cotta tiles and white lounge chairs.

In the kitchen I find the same black granite countertops and the same stainless steel appliances Mom was jealous of after

I blabbed about them following my first visit down here. I still think she sent me down to spy on him that time.

But I did feel sorry for her since she didn't have any of these "luxuries." It didn't seem fair—not to her or me. Now I check the contents of the fridge and wonder if Dad's help-yourself policy applies to the six-pack of Corona. Not that I'd go there— I most definitely would not. But I do know Mom would have a hissy fit if she knew. Instead I take a Coke, then dig around the mostly empty cabinets until I find a bag of Cheetos. If Mom could see me now.

Satisfied that I've sufficiently cased the joint, I set to work unpacking my things. Unfortunately, Dad didn't have time to clear his junk out of the guest room, which is now my room, but he told me I could put it in the storage closet off the back terrace. Of course, the storage closet is full—at least it seems full on first appearance—but with a little rearranging I can make room for his things. By the time I'm done, it's so stuffed I barely get the door closed.

Now I set to work putting my room in order. First I set up the old computer. Dad gave it to me right before he left Mom. I wasn't sure if it was because he didn't want to pack the bulky thing up or if he thought he was being generous. But I'd really rather have a laptop. Next I hang up my clothes, and when I run out of hangers, I sneak into his room to see if he has any extras.

Finally, I see something that's changed. He's gotten himself a real set of bedroom furniture! It's made of sleek-looking dark wood in a contemporary design, with a king-sized bed. Naturally, this makes me curious. Why does a single man need a *king*-sized bed? However, it's none of my business. Like we agreed, we will treat each other with respect and act like adults. I study a painting above the bed. It looks kind of Italian with rich tones of red, gold, and black, and it's obviously not an original. But in a way, it's attractive. I bend down and touch the garnet red velvety bedspread. Is this really my dad's taste? Or is he trying to be someone or something else? In some ways this all seems like such a stereotype. Really, he could've done better.

I stand there for a long time, just looking at this foreign world, comparing this space to the bedroom my parents used to share—and the difference is extreme. I would describe their old room as painfully traditional and boring, with a floral bedspread and pastel-colored pillows and too many ruffles and my mom's porcelain knickknacks on every flat surface. I suppose it's not a surprise that Dad decided to go in the exact opposite decor direction.

Suddenly I feel like an intruder and fear I may have just broken my "grown-up" agreement, but I still need hangers. Dad should understand. I ease open his closet and see his neatly hung clothes, arranged by color and style. My dad has always been a meticulous dresser. He even shines his shoes. My mom used to complain about the expense of his dry cleaning, claiming she could do his laundry at home and save them lots of money. But Dad insisted that dry cleaning was a business expense for him and if he didn't go to work looking like a *GQ* ad, his job might be in jeopardy. And since a lot of employees got laid off at the onset of the recent recession but Dad managed to get a transfer to an even better job, I suspect he was right.

I grab about twenty wire dry-cleaning hangers, close his tidy closet, and tiptoe from his room. I'm not sure what the tiptoeing is all about, but as I close the door, I decide I won't go trespassing in there again. It's just not very adultlike.

It's getting close to nine and my room's pretty much put together, but Dad is still not home and I'm getting hungry.

The Coke and Cheetos just aren't cutting it. I wonder about calling his cell and then realize his condo doesn't have a land-line. And, thanks to my mom, I don't have a cell phone. She was certain I would use a cell phone to secretly contact all the boys who were dying to date me. Hopefully Dad will see the sensibil-ity in me having one now. Especially since his condo is essen-tially cut off. What if I had an emergency?

Thinking of emergencies makes me concerned about my dad. He said he'd be home around eight and he promised to take us to dinner. What if something went wrong? What if he got in a car wreck? Or had a heart attack in the middle of a strenuous backhanded return? Oh, for a cell phone.

Instead of worrying, I scavenge through the kitchen again in search of something a little more substantial (and healthier) than my previous snack. Finally settling on a can of chicken noodle soup, I nuke it in the microwave and am just finishing it off when I hear the sound of someone at the door.

At first I jump, wondering what I'll do if it's a break-in. Should I grab a frying pan or something to defend myself? I'm just heading for the steak knife drawer when Dad walks in, looking all clean and happy.

"Hey, Hay," he calls out.

This is his old greeting for me, but somehow it doesn't charm me tonight. Not like it used to do. "Where were you?"

His smile fades. "Playing racquetball, remember?"

"Yes, I remember that, but you said you'd be home —" I stop myself, remembering our grown-up rules. "Never mind." I turn away from him and put my empty bowl in the sink.

"I'm sorry, Haley." He drops his bag by the door and comes over and places a hand on my shoulder. "My old buddy Tyson was there tonight and we had drinks afterward. I didn't think you'd mind." He points at the soup can still on the counter. "And it looks like you found something to eat."

I just nod with my back to him.

"So all's well?"

"Sure, Dad." I force a smile.

"Are you still hungry?"

I shrug.

Now he frowns. "I guess that wasn't very nice of me, running off on you on your first night here. But I thought you'd be busy settling in anyway."

"I was." I nod. "I got everything unpacked."

"So . . . how 'bout we order in pizza?"

Now my smile is genuine. "Sounds good."

We confer over what we like, he makes the call, and then we flop down in the living room, where he turns on a Raiders football game from last week saved in his DVR. I'm not really that much into football, but for Dad's sake I try to act interested. And he actually tries to teach me about what's going on with all those dudes in their skintight uniforms and spacey looking helmets. I'm actually starting to catch on by the time the pizza arrives. And by the time the game ends, I think I may have become a true Raiders fan.

By eleven Dad and I are both ready to call it a day. "I don't usually do much on Sundays," he tells me as we head to our rooms. "And I like to sleep in."

"That works for me." My hand is on the doorknob.

"I—uh—I forgot to tell you that I do have, well, kind of a girlfriend now, Haley."

"Oh . . ." I just nod like this is no big deal.

"Yeah. Estelle works with me. It's not real serious; in fact, we're actually just really good friends. But we usually spend the weekends together, so she'll probably expect me to do something with her tomorrow." He looks nervous. "Are you okay with that?"

Now I'm not really sure what "okay with that" means, but I just nod and try to act cool. "Sure, why not?"

He smiles. "You're a good kid, Haley."

"Thanks." Then we tell each other good night and I go into my room and try to wrap my head around this new development. Oh, it's not that I thought my dad wouldn't find someone else — or even that he'd be celibate. My mom had always been suspicious that he'd found someone else . . . long, long ago. She rationalized that was the reason for their marital difficulties.

In fact, I'm sure that's why she sent me down here when I was fourteen, just so I could spy on him and find out. But at the time I saw nothing to suggest Dad did anything besides go to work and come home. He didn't even play racquetball. When I reported this back to Mom, it almost seemed like she was disappointed, like it would have validated her in some twisted way to know he'd been cheating on her all along.

I may not be the worldliest girl, but I can put two and two together and I'm pretty sure, based on Dad's posh-looking bedroom, that he and Estelle are more than just friends. Maybe they're not actually sleeping together . . . yet. But I don't think someone like my dad puts that much effort into his bedroom unless he's hoping to entertain.

I can't bear to imagine what my mom would think if she had any idea about any of this. And now, as I get into my nightgown, I make a pact with myself. I will not keep second-guessing my life in regard to my mother. Obviously she hates all of this — no surprise there. She thinks Dad is the Devil and now, by association, I am evil too.

According to my mother, anyone who doesn't believe what she and her church believe is going to hell anyway. So, really, what's the use? Why try? It hasn't escaped my notice that if I am turning my back on my mom, I am probably turning my back on God as well. A small part of me isn't comfortable with that decision. But the larger part of me is so fed up that I seriously don't care. Why should I?

Oh, it's not that I plan to throw away all my morals and standards. For some reason, one that I don't fully understand and can't really explain, I still think I will take my abstinence pledge seriously. I pledged to remain pure until marriage at my mom's church when I was thirteen, right after the divorce, and at the time it felt very real and meaningful. I believe it's right to respect myself and my body. And I want to save myself until marriage. Because despite everything Mom has said to me, I do value myself and I do believe that true love is worth waiting for — mostly I think I am worth waiting for.

Even during my romance with Bryce (we only kissed, but sometimes it got intense), I made my stand, and he actually seemed to respect me for it. And I liked that. It gave me a sense of control . . . and peace. Therefore I do not intend to compromise on that particular commitment. Maybe it has to do with God, or maybe it has to do with me. I'm not even sure anymore. But I am sure of this — I am not going to let my mother's weird religiousness rule over me. I refuse to become as critical and judgmental and angry as she has become. From now on I will be my own person.

As I get my goody bag of personal products and hair stuff from the dresser, I see the light blue Bible sitting there, almost like it's waiting for me to pick it up and read it. But whether it's because of the way my mom has used her Bible as a sword, hacking into Dad and me and anyone else who disagrees with her, or because I'm simply feeling rebellious, I pick up the Good Book and shove it into the bottom drawer, burying it beneath some old jeans before I slam the door closed.

I so do not want to become my mother! I don't want to look down on my dad—I do not want to judge or criticize him. And when I meet his girlfriend, Stella—or whatever her name is—tomorrow, I will act totally cool, like I'm completely comfortable with whatever their relationship might be. Even if they make out on the couch or even go to bed together at the end of the day, I am not going to react.

As I go into the hall bathroom, my own personal bathroom—well, at least until Dad has guests (like his girlfriend)—I decide to adopt a new grown-up way of thinking. As I arrange my things on the counter, lining them up nice and neat, and as I brush my teeth, I decide my philosophy will become *laissez-faire*. It's something I remember from last year's history class. It's usually a political or economic term, French for "let it be" or something to that effect. But from now on I will do just that. I will let it be. I will *live and let live*. And I suspect that my dad will be greatly relieved by this. Hopefully my mother will never know.

I don't know why I couldn't sleep in late this morning, especially after not sleeping too well last night. Maybe it was the sunlight pouring through my east-facing window. Or maybe it was the call of the swimming pool down below. But at a little past nine, I'm in my swimsuit, wrapped in a beach towel, and, with my key in hand, heading downstairs for a morning swim.

It's weird, because I definitely have a spring in my step. It's like I'm in a different world today. I'm here in sunny California and it feels like I just came back to summer. Oregon in mid-October can be beautiful . . . or it can be gloomy and gray. When I left, it was damp and dreary . . . and a little depressing.

I test the temperature of the water, and seeing that it's comfortable, I drop my towel on a chair and dive in. Naturally, the water feels colder on my body than it did on my foot, but after a few strokes, I'm acclimated — and it feels good, refreshing, invigorating. I feel more alive right now than I've felt in a long time.

I used to be on swim team. Until I developed curves. That's when Mom decided it was "indecent to go around in a skimpy team suit for all those teenage boys to gawk at," but I still love to swim. Who knows, maybe I'll look into it again at my new school. Although I'm afraid I'd be too out of shape to really compete without too much humiliation.

Despite being out of shape, I easily swim for about an hour. Then I find a nice sunny spot where I park myself on a chaise lounge and soak up some sun, even falling asleep for a while.

When I wake up, I'm toasty warm and very thirsty. The clock on the fence says it's getting close to eleven and I'm guessing Dad might be up by now. I head back upstairs, unlock the door, and come into the condo in time to see a tangle of arms and legs on the black leather sofa. It takes me a couple of seconds before I realize it's my dad—and a blonde!

I turn my head away and, without saying a word, hurry past them. I'm not sure if they even saw me or not. With a pounding heart, I remind myself of my new laissez-faire attitude. *Let it go*, I tell myself as I turn on the shower. *Live and let live.* But, *cheese whiz*, I think as I vigorously shampoo my hair, *why couldn't they take their little act behind closed doors?* As I apply conditioner, I wonder about Stella or whatever her name is—how old is she? I swear she looked about my age, but then I couldn't really see her face—as it appeared superglued to my dad's face.

"Live and let live," I say out loud. "Just chill and let it go."

By the time I'm drying my hair, I feel a little calmer. And by the time I put a little curl into the ends—I'm not sure why even, but I suspect I'm just trying to delay the inevitable—I think I can handle this.

Finally, dressed and ready to face whatever it is that's waiting for me, I emerge from my room to the smell of something good cooking, which reminds me that I really am hungry.

"Hey, Hay," my dad hails. "Come and meet Estelle."

So it's Estelle, not Stella. I paste on a smile and go into the kitchen to see a very young-looking blonde woman stirring what looks like eggs. Dad does an introduction and, feeling conspicuous, I reach out and shake her hand. She looks a little surprised but shakes mine, too.

"Do you like omelets, Haley?" she asks brightly.

"Sure, but you don't have to cook for me."

"Estelle brought breakfast things over," Dad says. "She's a really good cook."

"You just pick out what you want in it," Estelle tells me. "There are mushrooms, green onions, and a bunch of other things by the sink. Just throw what you want in a bowl and bring it to me. I used to work in a resort restaurant where I had to pump these out for a waiting customer every couple of minutes."

I gather some things and take them to Estelle as she's sliding an omelet onto a plate for Dad. He leans over and plunks a kiss on the top of her head. "Thanks, babe."

Thanks, babe? I try not to wrinkle my nose in disgust, but I can't help but think I never saw him treating my mom like that. Still, I'm not going there.

I wait and watch as Estelle cracks and whips up the eggs, then pours them into the sizzling pan. She adds my ingredients, using a spatula to gently turn the edges of the omelet, lets it cook a bit longer, and finally slides it onto a plate. "Here you go, Haley. And there are blueberry muffins by the fridge."

"Thanks." I don't kiss her on top of her head. I grab a muffin and go over to sit by Dad at the breakfast bar.

"Isn't she something?" he says to me.

I just nod and say, "Uh-huh." I'm watching her as I eat. Barefoot and dressed in yellow shorts and a white tank top, she looks shorter than me, about five foot six I'd guess, but her tanned legs look long and slender for her height, and her figure is good. Really good. Plus she's got that kind of long blonde hair most girls seem willing to spend hours of breathing fumes at a salon to achieve. And she's pretty. Not drop-dead gorgeous, but definitely pretty. I glance over at Dad and I swear he's drooling as he watches her. Or maybe it's the eggs.

"This is yummy, Estelle."

She's coming over to join us now, setting her plate opposite Dad and me. "Well, I thought with Haley here, you might want to have a real breakfast." She sits down and gives him a coy grin. "Just don't expect this kind of treatment every Sunday."

My dad feigns disappointment. "Oh, just when I'd gotten my hopes up."

"Well, I suppose we could arrange something."

I can tell their banter is full of sexual innuendo—things no daughter should have to hear coming from her father and his girlfriend. So I decide to change the subject. "Are you from around here, Estelle, or a transplant like Dad?"

"I grew up just a few miles from here." She rolls her eyes. "I keep telling Gordon I don't understand why he wanted to live here in Mayberry."

"Because it's cheaper than Fresno," he offers.

"But is it worth it?" She holds her fork in the air. "I mean, like the restaurants." She looks at me. "There are two."

"Two?" I blink.

Dad laughs. "That's not true." He starts naming them off, including ones like McDonald's and Burger King.

"Those aren't restaurants," she says. "I'm talking about places you'd take your girl for dinner."

He nods. "Well, I suppose you're right. But there's more than two, Estelle."

"But they roll up the sidewalks by eight. And there's only one movie theater and—"

"At least it's a quad," he shoots back.

"With pathetic movies."

"Well, I've heard good things about the schools in this one-horse town. Haley should appreciate that." Dad glances at me.

Estelle gets a slightly wistful look now. "Yeah, Mitchell High is pretty good for a high school." She sighs as she forks into her eggs. "I had some good times there."

"When did you graduate?" I ask, hoping I'm not too obvious. But, seriously, I want to know—how old is she? In some ways, she doesn't seem much older than me.

She narrows her eyes slightly, like she's summing me up or perhaps offended by my question. "About ten years ago," she tells me evenly, almost with a challenge in her tone.

"Oh. Do you think it's changed much since then?" Hopefully this will smooth over my slightly impertinent question.

She shrugs. "I doubt it. My little brother goes there, and whenever I attend an event, it seems pretty much the same."

"So did you get all your classes online like I told you to do?" Dad asks me.

"I think so."

"I took care of all your fees and things," he says. "So you should be all set for Monday."

"Are you nervous about a new school?" Estelle asks.

Now I shrug. "I guess so."

"Hey, I should introduce you to Buck."

I frown. "Buck?"

"My baby brother."

Dad laughs. "*Baby brother* just doesn't sound right when you're describing Buck Anderson." He looks at me. "Buck is six foot four and outweighs me by a long shot."

"He's a defensive linebacker," Estelle explains. "And Mitchell has a really good football team this year."

"This town is big into football," Dad tells me.

I let out a groan.

"Hey, you were acting like you liked it last night when we watched the Raiders game from last week."

"Wasn't that a great game?" Estelle says.

With them discussing the Raiders game, I take my empty plate to the sink, rinse it, and place it in the dishwasher. I consider offering to clean up, but they seem to be lingering, and suddenly I feel even more out of place. "Thanks for breakfast, Estelle. It was nice to meet you, but I want to go catch up on some e-mails. Excuse me."

She smiles. "Someone raised you right, Haley." She elbows Dad. "I guess it wasn't you."

Dad lets out a moan.

"Actually, Dad was around for most of my life," I tell her. "It's only been three years since the divorce."

Estelle looks surprised. "Just three years?" she questions Dad.

"Well, the marriage was over long before that. But, yes, the divorce was about three years ago."

Now I excuse myself again and this time I leave. As I walk to my room, I realize that Estelle is probably closer to my age than to Dad's. And math isn't even my strong subject. I close the door to my room and sit at my computer, but the truth is I don't have e-mail to check. Most kids my age don't use e-mail. They text. But then they have cell phones. And that reminds me of something. So after about thirty minutes, I go back out and find them cleaning up. I offer to help, but they're nearly done.

"Dad?" I begin carefully.

"Yeah?" He's pouring himself a last cup of coffee.

"I don't have a cell phone and I'm wonder—"

"You don't have a cell phone?" Estelle looks shocked. "Seriously?"

I shake my head no.

"Haley's mom is, well, shall I say a bit conservative."

"You're sixteen, right?" Estelle is looking at me like I'm an alien.

"Yes."

"Have you ever had a cell phone?"

Again with the shake of the head.

"Do you know how to drive?" she asks.

"My mom wasn't comfortable with that either."

Estelle gives my dad an incredulous look. "What is wrong with your ex-wife, Gordon?"

"It's a long story."

"Well, someday I'd like to hear it." She tosses the wadded dish towel on the counter. "But I think it's high time you got this little girl a cell phone, *Daddy*."

Now my preference would've been for just Dad and me to go cell phone shopping, but instead I find myself in the backseat of Dad's SUV, listening as Estelle goes on about some scandal going on in their workplace. I'm really trying to like this woman, but something about her sets my teeth on edge. Still, I'm determined to act civilized and hide my true emotions.

Estelle takes over at the cell phone shop, telling me what I want and why I want it. She even pushes me to get a hot pink phone—and I hate hot pink. But when we leave, there is a hot pink phone in my bag. I wonder if I can paint it. Maybe if I sanded it a little, my acrylic paints would stick. I study the phone and imagine how I can make it look really cool. Estelle continues to chatter away at my dad. As she goes on about a fashion-challenged coworker, I make a mental list of all the things I hate about this chick:

- She is too young for Dad. If he'd been a teenaged father, she could easily be his child.
- She is superficial.
- She thinks she's hot. I caught her checking herself out in the mirror several times, and she always seems pleased with what she sees.
- She's catty.
- Even worse than catty, she's a serious gossip. If her boss could hear her right now, she'd probably be out of a job.
- She isn't very smart. Already she's misused or mispronounced at least three words.
- She treats me like a child. I think this is what I hate most of all.

I'm just finishing my list when I see that we're on the freeway. "Where are we going?"

"Didn't you hear Estelle saying she wanted to do some shopping?"

"Uh, no . . ."

"You don't mind, do you?" Dad glances at Estelle uneasily.

"You might want to do some shopping too." Estelle turns around in the seat and peers at me. "I mean, you are starting at a new school tomorrow, and from what I've heard, your mom isn't big into fashion, right?"

"Not much."

"I thought Estelle might be able to help you out, baby doll." Dad sounds hesitant. "She's pretty fashion conscious and tuned in to younger styles."

I look at her tank top and wonder.

She laughs. "Oh, I don't always dress like this, but it was hot today. And to be honest, I only thought I was coming over to make breakfast."

"Uh-huh." I just nod. I'm fully aware that I'm acting like a brat — totally unlike what I'd planned to be like.

"But if you're not interested" — Dad is moving into the right lane — "there's an exit ahead. I can turn around and take you home."

"Oh, come on, Haley. Admit you need some clothes and maybe even a little fashion advice." Estelle laughs. "For Pete's sake, your dad is offering you clothes — what girl passes up an opportunity like that?"

Her reasoning registers with me. "Yeah, you're right. I could use some things. Sure, let's go shopping."

We end up at this chic little outlet mall where Dad immediately bows out. He hands me a gold credit card and grabs his iPad. "I'm off to Starbucks for a mocha and to check the stock market. See you later."

Estelle acts like this is perfectly acceptable. Then, practically taking me by the hand and acting like she knows this mall like the back of her own hand, she drags me to her favorite shops, and something tells me this whole "spur-of-the-moment" shopping trip was totally premeditated.

However, when I see my image in a full-length mirror at the Gap, I realize that perhaps I really did need a style intervention. There's no denying that Mom was not only "not into fashion" but vehemently opposed to most trends, especially if she deemed them provocative. If she could've dressed me like a nun or Laura Ingalls, she wouldn't have hesitated.

I stand here taking inventory of my baggy Lee jeans and sports T-shirt. If I stuffed my long dark hair under a ball cap, I might be able to pass for a guy. To be fair, I don't always dress like this. I used to try to compensate for Mom's fashion phobia by adapting clothes into funkier designs and/or shopping at secondhand shops with my babysitting money.

Occasionally I'd come up with something good and sneak out of the house wearing it, but if I got caught, my remodeled clothes were confiscated and a huge fight would ensue. So most of the time I just told myself that clothes didn't really matter and that things like art and music and getting good grades were more important. Now I wonder.

"These jeans would look great on your long legs." She holds up the latest style in jeans—the kind my mom would have a cow over. Maybe I'm just weak or maybe I want to thumb my nose in Mom's face, but I take the jeans from Estelle, and after several tries and size changes, I decide on a pair. And I have to admit, they look awesome.

I'm not sure if it's the jeans or Estelle's influence, but it feels like something in me was triggered when I put them on, and so, like a fashion junkie, I let Estelle take me to more stores—picking up more clothes and shoes and even makeup. After a couple of hours and burdened down with bags and a credit card that should've melted by now, we go to find Dad.

"How'd it go?" he asks with a slightly worried expression.

"I think you've created a monster." I hold up fistfuls of shiny shopping bags and grin. "Hope you're good with that."

He looks doubtful. "This won't be a regular thing, will it?"

"I hope not," I admit. "But you guys were probably right; my wardrobe was pretty pathetic. Thanks!"

My first day at my new school was unremarkable. Well, except for meeting a certain guy I cannot get out of my head.

It all started when Estelle's "baby brother," Buck Anderson, took it upon himself to become my personal guide today, although for clarification's sake, Buck is not the guy who's stuck in my head. He was merely the connection. For some reason, which I'm sure is named Estelle Anderson, Buck decided to become my new best friend. It was a little awkward at first — me hanging with a guy who resembles a Mack truck — but I suppose I appreciated it on some level.

Even so, the jock and cheerleader crowd has never been my cup of tea, and that is the table I sat with at lunchtime. But I was polite, and I was also myself. I let it be known I was more into art and music than sports. I figured those kids could take it or leave it. Because there's no way, even if I'm dressed like them, that I'll conform to fit into their world. I suspect by tomorrow they won't even remember my name.

Although I have to admit that I did enjoy the banter and liveliness of this group, and I was probably a bit envious of friendships that seemed fairly sturdy. But the part that sticks with me was this one particular guy. As soon as he joined the group, I could barely take my eyes off him. Not that he noticed me. But I can say, as an artist, that Harris Stephens is the most gorgeous guy I've ever laid eyes on. With dark curly hair, which seems a tad long for a sports jock (he's a quarterback), and dreamy dark blue eyes and a straight nose and serious lips and a slender but great physique (muscles seem to be the one thing athletic kids have over most art and music geeks), what girl wouldn't drool a bit?

Naturally, Harris already has a girlfriend. Not that I had any psychotic delusions that I'd ever have a chance with a guy like that. But I suppose a girl can dream. However, it's a bit dismaying that his girlfriend is such a cliché. I hate thinking that, too, especially since I was so determined *not* to be judgmental. But his girlfriend, Emery Morrison, is a bouncy, effervescent strawberry-blonde cheerleader, and from what I can tell, she is everyone's very best friend.

As I read in a book once, this girl is so sweet that sugar wouldn't melt in her mouth. The homecoming queen election posters plastered all over the school bore testimony to her vast popularity. It seems Emery has Mitchell High in the palm of her perfectly manicured hand. And, really, she can have all that. I just wish she'd leave the boy with me.

I was so obsessed with fantasizing about Harris Stephens that the afternoon went by in a hazy blur. This is unfortunate considering how much I'd been looking forward to art class right after lunch. As I walk home from school, all I can remember from art is that a couple of kids — Poppie and Zach I think their names were — seemed fairly nice, like potential friend material. But I was so smitten by Harris that I can't even remember what Poppie and Zach looked like.

On my second day of school, I'm surprised Buck is still hanging around me, still acting like we're friends . . . or is it family? As a result I end up sitting at his friends' table again. And this time Harris Stephens actually looks my way.

"Are you new?" he asks.

Emery laughs. "Don't you remember her from yesterday?"

He shrugs, eying me carefully. "Not really."

"That's Haley McLean."

I'm surprised she remembers my name, but then that's kind of like her job I suppose. "That's okay," I tell Harris. "I'm not really very memorable."

He tilts his head to one side. "I wouldn't say that."

Now I laugh.

"Harris is terrible at remembering faces," Emery tells me in a confidential tone. "I think he has some kind of disorder."

"I do not," he shoots back. "It's just that I'm not obsessed with knowing everyone and their great-aunt Betty in this entire school." He jerks his thumb at Emery. "Because I, unlike some people, am not *running* for anything."

"Oh, Harris." She makes a pout.

"So where are you from, Haley?" Harris asks. I think he's only giving me attention to irritate Emery, but I don't mind and I tell him Oregon.

"I've been up there before," he says with enthusiasm. "What a great place. I wouldn't mind living there."

Now I start to go on about how great it is, talking like I'm head of the Oregon tourist department (is there such a thing?), but Harris still seems really interested. He even talks about the colleges up there, mentioning how they've had some pretty hot football teams.

I'm so nervous that it's hard to eat my lunch, but I pretend to . . . and I pretend I'm not nervous either.

"So what are you into, Haley?"

I just stare at him, thinking, *I'd like to be into you*, but there's no way I would say something so lame. "Oh, art and music."

"Music?" He looks interested. "What kind?"

"I play guitar, write songs, mostly for myself."

"I'll bet you hope to become the next Taylor Swift," Saundra Ketchum spouts, and everyone laughs like this is a great joke. Saundra is Emery's best friend, the real one, but she strikes me as an insecure snob, and of all the kids at this table, I probably like her the least. But hearing her take a jab at me is a good reminder that despite Buck's best efforts, I do not belong here.

"I actually like Taylor Swift," I tell Saundra.

This just makes her laugh harder.

"You know, I like Taylor Swift too."

Now everyone looks at Harris like he's just sprouted a second head.

"I do," he argues. "She's talented."

"You know, I kind of like her too," Emery admits.

Saundra lets out a groan. "Give me a break."

"You can laugh at Taylor Swift if you want to," I say. "She probably laughs all the way to the bank."

Several of them are arguing now—is Taylor Swift really talented or is she a geek? But Harris turns back to me. "What kind of music do you write and play?"

I shrug. "I'm not sure it's a real genre, but I suppose it's a mix of folk and R & B and sometimes a little jazz." I smile. "I'm kind of eclectic."

He nods. "Sounds interesting."

"Are you into music?"

He glances around the table, like he doesn't want to say anything.

"Or maybe jocks don't get into things like that," I tease. "It might mess with your game."

"Actually, I was just learning guitar, but my playing has kind of plateaued. I should probably take lessons."

"Oh . . . ?" Right, he would be into guitar. Now I'll probably fall completely in love.

"Hey, it sounds like you're pretty good. Do you ever give lessons?"

This could be my chance and I don't want to blow it. "Lessons?" I act like I'm pondering this. "I suppose I could give lessons. I mean, I've been playing guitar since I was twelve and I've had lessons." I shrug. "Yeah, I guess I would consider it."

"What?" Emery tunes back in to our conversation. "What are you two hatching here?"

So Harris explains that he's wanted to take guitar lessons and that I'm willing to teach him.

"Really?" Emery looks dubiously at me. "*You* teach guitar lessons?"

"Not usually, but I'm open to it."

She turns back to Harris. "Between football practice and games, when do you think you'll have time to take guitar lessons? Or practice, for that matter?"

He frowns at her. "You're sounding more and more like my mom, Emery. Seriously, that could get old."

Emery's eyes get clouded now and I can tell she's hurt. I actually feel a little bit sorry for her. "Well, excuse me," she says in a terse tone. She picks up her purse, nudges Saundra, and the two of them walk off.

"Here we go." Harris rolls his eyes. "Time for drama club."

"Good thing Emery didn't hear you say that," Buck teases.

"Sorry, but I get tired of being treated like Emery's little boy," Harris says to the others at the table.

"What about when she tucks you in and kisses you good night?" Cal Jorgenson laughs. From what I can tell Cal and Harris are pretty good friends.

Harris winks at him. "There's a time and a place for mothering."

So more jokes are made about guys and girls and I am feeling extremely uncomfortable. Fortunately the lunch hour is about over, so I stand to leave too.

"What about those guitar lessons?"

I turn to Harris. "You're still interested?"

He nods. "Yeah, there's more to life than playing football."

This provokes more teasing and bawdy jokes from the jock dudes, who act like the sun rises and sets over the goalposts. During their friendly banter, I write my cell phone number on a corner of notebook paper and slip it to Harris. "If you're serious about lessons, give me a call."

Our eyes lock and he nods again.

I feel slightly faint as I stand back up, but I simply smile and tell him, "Later." Then with trembling knees, I walk away, managing to get all the way out the cafeteria door without collapsing. I cannot believe what just happened. Or maybe nothing happened. By the time I'm nearly to the art room, I'm starting to giggle.

I gave Harris Stephens my phone number—how crazy is that?

"What's so funny?" a girl with magenta hair asks me as I enter the room.

"Huh?" I look at her, trying to remember who she is.

"Why are you laughing?" she repeats.

"Laughing?"

"Oh, never mind." She gives me an exasperated look.

"You're Poppie, right?"

Now she smiles. "Yep. That's me."

"I didn't realize I was laughing. I guess I was amused."

"Obviously."

"Okay, fine, the reason I'm laughing is because I just gave Harris Stephens my phone number."

She looks shocked. "You gave Harris Stephens your number?"

My hand goes over my mouth. I can't believe I just told her that. What is wrong with me?

"Oh, it's okay; it's not like I'll tell anyone," she says as we sit at the same worktable. "But why on earth did you give that boy your phone number?"

"He wants to take guitar lessons."

She looks even more surprised now.

"Never mind," I tell her. "I'm sure he'll never call. His girlfriend says he's too busy to play guitar anyway."

"So you teach guitar lessons?"

"I haven't, but I suppose I could."

Now a tall, thin guy comes over and sits at our table too. He's got shoulder-length wavy brown hair and wire-rimmed glasses. "Hey," he says as he opens his portfolio. "What's up?"

"Haley is giving Harris Stephens guitar lessons," Poppie blurts out.

"You said you wouldn't say any—"

"Sorry." She holds up her hands. "But don't get your knickers in a wad. Zach won't tell anyone."

"You're giving Harris Stephens guitar lessons?" Zach peers at me like I'm from another planet.

"No," I say loudly. "I never even said that." I turn to Poppie. "I told you he asked me about lessons and I gave him my phone number. That is all."

"Oh, you gave him your phone number?" Zach says this like it's something sleazy.

I glare at him. "Is there a law against giving out phone numbers at this school?"

"No, no," he says smoothly. "Just as long as you know who you're giving them to."

"What's that supposed to mean?" I whisper since Ms. Flores is going to the head of the class.

"Nothing . . . but if you're handing out your phone number to every Tom, Jerk, and Harry, how about giving it to me, too?"

I turn away from him now, pretending to focus on Ms. Flores as she talks about an upcoming art fair, asking for volunteers. Both Poppie and Zach raise their hands, but I keep mine on the table.

"There will be extra credit given," she adds, "and for those preparing their portfolios for college, I should point out that this will look good in your bios."

I hesitantly lift my hand, along with several reluctant others. I'm not even sure why I feel this is such an imposition. Last year I would've jumped at an opportunity like this. But suddenly I feel torn and distracted—I'm thinking about Harris and his friends and wondering if he's really going to call me about guitar lessons and whether or not I could possibly fit into that crowd and if I could fit, would I really want to? If it meant belonging to Harris, I know I would.

As I get back into a sketch I started yesterday, something I plan to paint with watercolors, I realize that I'm changing and I'm afraid there isn't much I can do about it.

"So are you pretty good on guitar?" Zach asks me.

"Huh?" I look up, trying to process this question. Is he teasing me again, or is he serious?

"If you're offering to give lessons, I assume you must be good." He's studying me closely through those wire rims.

I shrug. "I'm okay."

"I play guitar too."

I give him an even look. "Why does that not surprise me?"

Now he seems surprised. "I don't know, why?"

"Maybe it's this John Lennon image you're sporting," I say glibly.

Poppie lets out a laugh so loud it sounds like a snort. "Good one, Haley."

"I happen to admire John Lennon," Zach says. "As a musician anyway."

"So do I, but I don't go around trying to imitate him."

Poppie giggles.

"And neither do I." Zach adjusts his glasses. "Contacts irritate my eyes and I was getting sick of those dark plastic frames. I figured I'd try something new."

I can tell I've hurt his feelings and that makes me sad. "Actually, I think it's a good look, Zach. Very cool."

"Really?" He sounds hopeful.

"Uh-huh. I was just getting back at you for tweaking me about Harris."

He leans toward me. "You're not really into Harris Stephens, are you?"

"No, of course not." I shake my head. "But what difference would it make if I was?"

He gets a grim look. "If you were, I would warn you."

"Warn me?"

He nods as he licks the tip of his pencil.

"Zach would warn you to stay away from Harris because Zach is crushing on you. He wants to keep you to himself, Haley." Poppie says this loud enough for a few others to hear, and now half the class erupts into giggles and my cheeks grow warm.

"Poor Poppie," Zach says in a pseudo soothing tone, "feeling a bit jealous, are we?"

"Get over yourself!" Poppie gets up and goes across the room, presumably to get paintbrushes but I think she's just embarrassed.

"What was that all about?" I ask quietly.

"Poppie and I used to be a couple," he explains while he continues drawing. "The breakup was perfectly congenial, but I sometimes think she's still into me."

"And you're not into her?"

"Not so much." He looks up and smiles, and I realize he actually has an attractive smile. And, really, he's much better looking than John Lennon. I suppose if someone like Harris Stephens wasn't out there walking the earth, a guy like Zach might be interesting to me. Except that I have this sneaking suspicion he's a Christian.

Not that he acts like one exactly. But I noticed he had some images of crosses as well as a Jesus fish sketched in his notebook—and I'm just not going there. No way. Besides, I just can't seem to shake Harris out of my head.

I find it hard to believe I'm still welcome in Harris's crowd. It's like no one even questions me hanging with them, so I keep coming back. I'm fully aware that there's one main reason I keep coming back — a six-foot-tall handsome hunk of a reason.

So far no one seems to suspect my real motive, since no one is questioning me. That might be because I'm playing my hand very carefully. I go out of my way to be congenial to Emery; I'm even tolerant with Saundra — although I have no authentic respect for her. In my previous life, I would have categorized her as a mean girl. Yet, somehow, she doesn't really scare me now.

Even so, I can't get over the feeling that I'm an imposter here, or perhaps I'm playing a game or just waiting for the other shoe to fall . . . or maybe the boot. Finally it's Friday and nothing has come along to derail me from my charade of fitting in with the "in" crowd, and I almost believe I'm really part of it. This fills me with a strange mix of emotions, contradictory things like pride and angst and shame.

"I never would've taken you for one of them," Poppie says as we select watercolor brushes for our current projects. She's just been lecturing me on why the kids I've been hanging with are all wrong for me.

"Why is it that just because you're friends with someone, everyone assumes you've become one of them?" I shoot back. "Why can't I just be me?"

She gives me a long, curious look. "Good question. Why *can't* you just be yourself?"

"How do you even know who I am? You've known me for all of one week."

She just shrugs and goes back to our worktable.

"I have to side with Poppie on this," Zach says from behind me. I didn't even know he was listening.

"Why?" I demand.

"Maybe we see something you're missing." He adjusts his wire rims and peers at me.

"Like what?"

"Like you're obviously a square peg trying to squeeze yourself into a round hole."

"What's that supposed to mean?"

"When you're with the others — the so-called cool group — you're not yourself."

"See, there you go, acting like you know who I am. Just like Poppie. You've known me a week and yet you know who I am?"

"Let me put it like this, Haley. You're one person in here with us and a totally different person out there with them."

I think about this. "Well, maybe I'm acting different with you guys in here, just trying to fit in. Did you ever think of that?"

He chuckles. "You pull it off really well then. You're totally believable in here. But out there you look like a farce."

"A farce?" Do Zach and Poppie sit in the cafeteria just staring at me throughout the entire lunch hour? Maybe they're spies for my mom.

"You're like a caricature of them, Haley. Like you're trying too hard, trying to pass yourself off as being like them, when it's obvious you're not."

I know what he's saying is true, yet I have no intention of showing that. Mostly I feel aggravated that my disguise is so easy to see through. If Zach and Poppie have figured me out, why haven't the others? Or maybe they have and they're just waiting to pull the rug out from under me.

Whatever the case, I feel seriously rattled as I gather my things after school. Questions like *Who am I?* are rolling around in my head, and I can't wait to get out of here.

"Hey, wait up," calls a guy.

I turn to see Harris coming toward me. I make a sheepish wave and slam my locker shut, glancing around to see if Emery or any of her friends are nearby. This could be the setup.

"I've been looking for you since lunch." He leans against my locker. "I wanted to see if you're still on for my guitar lessons."

"Seriously?" I frown at him.

"Yeah, I want to learn to play. Are you into that or not?"

I make an uneasy smile. "Sure, but what about Emery? She seemed a little concerned—"

"Emery is not my mother." He looks over his shoulder like he doesn't want anyone to hear this. "The truth is, I'm about to break up with her."

This makes me feel slightly dizzy . . . and suspicious. "Really?"

"Don't say anything though." He looks into my eyes and that makes me even dizzier. "I feel like I can trust you, Haley. You seem different than the other girls. More mature, you know?"

I just shrug.

"So anyway, how about tomorrow afternoon for lessons?"

"Sure," I tell him. Then I give him my dad's address.

"Hey, that's not far from where I live. Cool."

I nod. "Yeah. Cool."

"Are you coming to the game tonight?"

Now I'm gauging . . . is this a casual question or a cloaked invitation? "I don't know."

He frowns. "You're not into football?"

I think hard and then decide to go for it, making my flirtiest smile. "I suppose I *could* be into football. I mean, if the right guy was playing."

He throws his head back and laughs. "Then you better get yourself to the game tonight."

Keeping up my sly, flirty persona, I just nod. "I'll give that some serious thought, Harris."

He pats me on the shoulder. "You do that, Haley."

As he leaves, my head is spinning and I feel tingles from the roots of my hair to my toenails. He is coming on to me— I know it. And he said he's going to break up with Emery. It's like Harris Stephens is mine for the taking. And I'm going to do the taking. This is a chance I do not want to miss. I am most definitely going to the game! Hopefully Dad won't mind.

I practically dance all the way home, and once I'm there, I spend the afternoon trying on every outfit I think would be perfect for going to a football game. And I primp and primp.

"Hello," Dad calls out as he gets home.

Bracing myself for his disappointment, I go out and try to think of a gentle way to break the news that I want to go to the game tonight.

"Hey, Hay." He grins. "How's it going?"

"Great. How about you?" I realize how little Dad and I have talked this week. He works such long hours that he's sometimes getting home just as I'm getting ready for bed, and it feels like we're ships in the night.

"Okay." Now his grin fades. "Hey, you don't mind if I take Estelle out tonight, do you? It's kind of an expected thing, but I could cancel if you—"

"No, Dad," I say quickly. "That's actually perfect because I wanted to go to the football game anyway."

His smile returns. "Great!" Now he looks more closely at me. "You look really pretty, Haley."

I give him a self-conscious thank-you and head back to my room. Hopefully he doesn't know that I'm fixing up for a boy. Of course, Dad probably wouldn't even care. It's Mom who flips out over something like this.

"Don't wait up for me," Dad says as he's getting ready to leave. "I might be in late."

"Okay." I just nod.

"Have fun!" He jingles his car keys and, just like that, he's gone. I feel a strange sense of detachment as I stand there by myself in the condo—kind of like I'm all alone in the universe. On one hand, I should be thankful for this newfound freedom. On the other hand, it's a bit unsettling.

It's still light when I walk to the game. A car full of guys honks at me and offers me a lift, but there's no way I'm climbing in with a bunch of strangers, thank you very much. I feel a little odd going to the game by myself. The stands aren't that crowded, and I soon discover that this is the junior-varsity game and in its second half.

Some of the varsity cheerleaders are among the spectators, but I don't see Emery or Saundra among them. However, Libby Farnsworth, one of Emery's lesser friends, waves me over to join them. Libby isn't a cheerleader but is part of their crowd. And in my opinion, she's one of the nicer ones.

"Did you hear the news?" she urgently asks me.

"What news?" A rush of panic hits me—did something terrible happen to Harris? Car wreck, broken bones, what is it?

"Emery and Harris broke up," she says dramatically.

Concealing my true emotions with a serious expression, I slowly nod, trying to take this in. "Oh, that's too bad," I finally say, but in reality I am controlling myself from doing the happy dance. "What happened?"

"I guess we should've expected it. They've been fighting a lot lately and we all know what that means. Emery is saying it was mutual."

"Yeah, right," Deidre Thornton says as she joins us. Deidre is a cheerleader and one of Emery's closer friends. "Emery's been home crying her eyes out all afternoon." Deidre holds up her phone. "Saundra just texted me saying Emery might not even make it to tonight's game. And we really need her to do our new formation."

"That's too bad," I say for the second time. Inside I'm cheering and clapping my hands. Outside I look as disturbed as these two.

"It might be for the best," Deidre concedes. "Emery hasn't been that happy with Harris since last summer." She glances at Libby. "Remember?"

Libby nods. "Oh, yeah. I almost forgot."

"What happened?" I ask innocently.

"Emery thinks Harris cheated on her," Deidre says. "Naturally, Harris denied it."

"And Emery didn't have any solid evidence," Libby adds. "So I think she decided to overlook it."

Suddenly someone scores a touchdown and everyone is yelling and cheering; figuring it's our school's team, I cheer too—with abandon. Mostly I'm cheering for the breakup of Harris and Emery. It seems wrong in some ways, but it's not like they were married. Besides, Harris gave me the heads-up this afternoon. It takes all my self-control not to admit this to these two girls now. Instead, I stand there with them, pretending to be the biggest football fan ever while we wait for the JV game to end. Fortunately our team wins and there's even more opportunity for celebrating—and I really feel like celebrating.

"Want to get a bite to eat?" Libby says to me as the cheerleaders head down to the turf to join the JV rally in a victory yell. "I never had dinner tonight."

Thankful to have a person to hang with, I gladly agree, and as we head down to the concession area, she tells me a little more about the breakup between Emery and Harris. "Can you believe it? He didn't even do it in person. He broke up with her on the phone."

"Seriously?" I try not to look too happy. "That's a little harsh."

"Maybe . . . but you didn't see Emery storming off when he tried to talk to her after school. She wouldn't even listen to him."

"Why did Emery storm out?" I ask cautiously as I squirt mustard on my hot dog.

"Just a fight, I think." Libby sticks a straw in her soda. "They have them fairly regularly."

"Oh . . ."

We go back to the stands and I'm trying not to obsess over what is a real possibility—was the fight over me? Did Emery see him talking to me? Did he tell her he was coming to my house for guitar lessons tomorrow? Or am I just being paranoid?

We sit in the stands, eating our makeshift meal, and I try not to worry about all this as I watch the cheerleaders down there doing routines and trying to get the pregame crowd excited about the upcoming game. The jazz band is here in full force and Zach is part of it, playing trombone and wearing a goofy hat. So much for his John Lennon image.

Finally, it's time to announce the team, and I feel slightly breathless as I hear Harris Stephens's name over the loudspeaker. "A senior this year, starting quarterback . . ." The statistics echo meaninglessly through my head as I look down at him in his black and gold uniform. Who knew football players looked so hot in their uniforms? I stare directly at him and I could swear he's looking straight back at me. I even smile and he smiles back. I am in heaven!

Okay, this would not be my mom's definition of heaven by any means. In fact, if she could read my mind right now, she'd probably have the exact opposite place lined up for me. Because I am imagining myself kissing him. That's right — K-I-S-S-I-N-G! And the warmth that fills me is almost overwhelming. But I try to act natural.

The opposing team kicks off and I follow Libby's reactions as each play unfurls, but the whole time my eyes are on Harris — and Harris only. Whether he's on the field and I'm watching in trepid fear, hoping he doesn't get injured, or if he's on the sidelines and I'm staring at his back, at the number on his shirt. My new lucky number is eight! I cannot take my eyes off that boy!

By the time the game ends — and we win — I am a raving lunatic football fan, yelling, "We're number one! Tigers are number one!"

"Come on!" Libby grabs my arm. "What are you waiting for?"

Just like that, we, along with a bunch of others, are pouring onto the field, which is apparently okay, and congratulating the players. To my surprise, Buck Anderson comes over and gives me a big bear hug, lifting me right off the ground.

"Great game!" I gasp as he sets me back down on the turf.

"Thanks! You coming to the celebration party?"

"I . . . uh . . . I don't know . . ." I see Harris coming my way now. At least I hope he is, but since Emery is in between us, I'm not sure how this will go down. But he just gives her a stony look, barely tipping his head, then moves past her and—to my utter amazement—comes over to me.

"Glad you could make it, Haley."

Buck looks surprised, glancing from me to Harris like he's adding this up.

"Great game," I tell him, wishing for something wittier to say.

"Thanks."

Now I give him my flirty smile. "You make watching football fun."

Harris laughs. "Thanks."

"Sorry to hear about your breakup," I say loudly.

"Really?" His voice is lower.

I shrug. "Well, I'm sure it's difficult, you know, after being together for so long."

He slips an arm around me, giving me a sideways squeeze, the way my brother used to do when he was okay. "You're all right, Haley."

I giggle. "Thanks."

"Wait for me outside the locker room, okay?"

I feel another dizzying rush going to my head as I nod. "Okay."

As I walk back to the bleachers with Libby, I want to pinch myself. This has to be a dream—a really great dream. And I do not want to wake up!

CHAPTER 6

"**W**hat's going on with you and Harris?" Libby asks with a slightly suspicious look.

"Nothing," I assure her. "I mean, other than being friends. And I'm going to give him guitar lessons."

Deidre's brows arch. *"Really?"* Her voice is laced with skepticism.

I giggle nervously. "Is there a problem with that?"

Deidre just shakes her head, then hurries over to where Emery is huddled with friends, probably giving her their condolences.

But Libby stays with me, studying me with a dubious expression. "Hopefully you're not getting into some kind of a rebound romance with Harris."

I act startled. "A rebound romance?"

She just nods.

I force a laugh. "I seriously don't think so."

As we walk down the steps from the stadium, I make more small talk with Libby. Emery, encircled by a cluster of her closest friends, is making a dramatic exit. I almost expect the clog of girls to hoist her to their shoulders and carry her out — like she's the hero or some kind of victim.

I do not react to this little scene, not one way or another. Let them enjoy their drama. I have other things to be thinking about.

Since I came to the game alone, it's easy to slip out alone. I tell Libby good-bye, then hurry toward the gym. Trying to be as inconspicuous as possible, I go over and wait near the exit of the men's locker room. First I pretend to get a long drink from the water fountain. Then I carefully read the bulletin board, including (ugh!) a flyer about who to call if you think you have an STD. Keeping one eye on the door and jolting inwardly every time it opens and a guy steps out, I pretend to be texting on my phone. Until finally Harris emerges.

"Hey, you waited for me." He says this like he didn't expect me to be here.

"Sure. I figured you might need someone to talk to after your big breakup today."

He frowns. "I'd rather not talk about *that*, if you don't mind."

I grin. "I don't mind at all. By the way, did I tell you that was a great game?"

He nods. "You and everyone else." Now he slips his arm around my waist, not in a brotherly way this time, and guides me out the door and over to the parking lot. "I've been thinking about you all week, Haley." He opens the passenger door of his car—a sleek-looking black Nissan.

"Really?" I slip into the seat, feeling my heart pounding with excitement.

"Uh-huh." He closes the door, then hurries over to the driver's side.

I glance across the parking lot and notice there are still some kids milling around, but none of his or Emery's closest friends seem to be here. Still, I'm sure the word will get out that I'm with him. For all I know someone is texting Emery right this second. But as Harris drives out to the street (a bit too fast), I realize I do not care—not one bit. Let them talk all they want; I'm going to enjoy this. I almost feel like I'm on a roller coaster, like I plan to just hold on for the ride of my life.

"Ever since I first saw you," Harris tells me as he drives through town, "I wanted to get to know you better. At first I thought I was imagining it, but then I realized I was thinking about you constantly."

"Me, too," I quietly confess.

He turns to look at me. *"Really?"*

Now I wish I hadn't given that up so easily—what about my intentions to be coy and hard to get? "Well, sort of. I liked that you're into guitar . . . or at least you want to be."

He nods eagerly. "And I like that you're interested in more than just rah-rah-cheerleading or the state of your hair or how much you paid for your shoes. That gets so old."

I laugh. "I agree."

"Are you hungry?"

"A little." Okay, that is a big fat lie, but there's no way I'm going to say no when I'm certain he's probably starved after all that exercise.

"Well, everyone will be at Wet Willie's."

"What's that?"

"Just this old-fashioned hamburger joint. They've got the best burgers and shakes in town, but if you and I walk in there together, the jaws will drop and the tongues will flap and we'll be the hot topic for the evening."

"Oh . . ."

"If you want, we could go someplace—"

"No," I say quickly. "Wet Willie's is fine."

So he parks at the edge of a nearly full parking lot, and the next thing I know I'm trying to act perfectly natural as I walk into the crowded restaurant with Harris Stephens. To my relief, after the kids in there recover from the surprise, they seem to think nothing of us. This is high school. People break up and start over all the time. It's perfectly normal.

Harris looks disappointed when I only order a dinner salad. "Please, tell me you're not one of those anorexic girls who tries to live on greens and water," he says.

I laugh. "Not at all. It's just that I pigged out on a hot dog after the JV game, and I guess I'm not as hungry as I thought."

He nods like this is acceptable. Then our orders come, and as he eats, I try to keep the conversation going down a light and breezy track. It's actually a lot of fun talking to him. But then the restaurant gets even more crowded and several others come over to squeeze in with us, and I get lost in the banter and jokes bouncing around the booth.

"Come on." Harris grabs my hand. "Let's get out of this place. It's making my head hurt."

Relieved, I nod and go with him. "It was getting to me too."

The air outside feels cool and fresh, and we're halfway across the parking lot when Harris pulls me closer to him, ducks into a shadowy spot, then wraps his arms around me and gives me a very passionate and long kiss. It's like a scene from a romantic movie, and I could swear I am floating as I kiss him back.

"Sorry," he says a little breathlessly. "But I've been waiting all week to do that."

"Don't be sorry," I whisper, hoping my breath doesn't smell. I brushed my teeth three times before going to the game tonight, but after that hot dog, who knows?

Harris tugs me over to an even more private spot of the parking lot, pulling me close again. We kiss some more — and it's so amazing I wonder if I might actually faint.

"Oh, Haley, it's even better than I expected." He's running his fingers through my hair now, sending delightful tingles down my spine. "Do you know how soft your hair is?"

I giggle quietly. "No."

"Most girls get so much done to their hair that it can feel like straw, but yours is so silky and smooth . . . so natural." Then he's kissing me again.

"Hey, what's going on here?" demands a male voice, like someone's trying to play tough guy.

I look up to see Buck coming our way and cringe. What if he tells my dad?

"Hey, Buckie Boy." Harris grins at him. "You caught us."

Buck looks confused when he sees me with Harris, like he can't quite figure out how this happened.

"How's it going, Buck?" I try to sound casual. "Nice night, isn't it?"

He just nods. "Yeah. I guess." Then he continues on into the restaurant, and Harris and I laugh nervously.

"Buck's sister is my dad's girlfriend," I confess to Harris.

"So you and Buck are almost related." He laughs even harder now. "What does that make him? Like your stepbrother?"

I consider this. "Not exactly. But if Dad and Estelle got married, that would make him my uncle."

"Uncle Buck!" Harris hoots.

"Uncle Buck," I repeat, bursting into laughter.

"That's hilarious, Haley." He pulls me close to him again. "Have I told you how much fun you are to be with?"

"I don't think so." I'm looking up into his shadowy face. How is it possible to know a guy for just a few days and yet know you are in love—absolutely in love?

We eventually wind up back in his car and he drives us to a lookout point, which I suspect was created for couples to make out at. We sit up there, dividing our time between talking and laughing and kissing. But as time passes, we do more kissing than anything.

Harris's hands are moving around on me a lot too, and I try not to show it but it's making me nervous. This is further than I've ever gone with a guy, and I'm not even sure how to put the brakes on. Sometimes I try to use my hands to stop him and sometimes I just let him wander.

Suddenly a bright light shines into the car, and we both jump apart like we've been jolted by electricity.

Harris says a bad word as he reaches for the window switch. "It's the cops."

I straighten myself up, sitting upright in the seat as he puts the window down. "Hey there," Harris says in a friendly tone. "What's up?"

"What's up is you kids need to get home," the officer tells him. "But first I want to see your license and registration."

Harris obliges him, and I sit there holding my breath and imagining that the cop is going to call my mom.

The policeman hands Harris back his documents, then shines his light on me. "Does your mother know what you're doing, young lady?"

I force an innocent smile. "Not exactly."

He frowns. "Well, you both look like nice kids, so why don't you get on home before I change my mind and write you up."

"No problem." Harris nods and starts his engine.

"Whew," I say as he drives (slowly) away. "That was seriously freaky."

Harris just laughs. "Why?"

Now I consider my response. "I guess I was startled. Like I thought it was some crazed killer trying to break into the car, you know, like he wanted your car and money."

Harris nods with a more serious expression. "Yeah, that would be scary."

"I should probably get home anyway. My dad didn't expect me to be out this late."

"I'm getting tired too," he admits. "But are we still on for guitar lessons tomorrow?"

"Absolutely."

"And maybe we could go out afterward." He grins at me. "Like a real date."

I feign disappointment. "You mean this wasn't a *real* date?"

He laughs. "Oh yeah, I think it was a real date. A real good date."

At the condominium, Harris walks me up to the door and I suspect that, because the porch light is off, Dad isn't even home yet. However, I'm not comfortable asking Harris in, so I just pretend my dad's inside waiting for me as we share a final good-night kiss . . . and then a few more.

"See you tomorrow," I whisper.

"Yeah," he whispers back. "Tomorrow."

I wait for him to start down the stairs before I unlock the door. Then, like I'm walking on air, I float into the house. This whole evening has been so unreal—I feel like the luckiest girl on the planet.

As I get ready for bed, I wonder what Dad means by "late." It's nearly midnight and he's still not home. But I'm not too concerned. Mostly I'm still floating and I plan to have some really delicious dreams tonight.

It's after four when something wakes me up. It sounds like someone is breaking into the condo, and I quietly slip out of my bed and try to find my bag and my phone, getting ready to dial 911, when I realize it might be Dad. So I creep over to my door, which I've left cracked open, and peek through the slit to see Dad tiptoeing down the hallway to his room. I consider saying something, then remember our grown-up pact and just go back to bed. If he wants to stay out until four in the morning, it's none of my business.

Later that morning, I'm not surprised that Dad is sleeping in. I get myself a bowl of cold cereal and check my phone to see if Harris has texted me. I'm still getting comfortable with the whole texting thing, but it's kind of fun. To my dismay there is nothing. I consider taking a swim, but the weather seems to be cooling down. So I just sit, looking out the window and daydreaming about Harris. I can't wait to see him again. This reminds me of our guitar lesson, so I get out my guitar, tune it, and spend some time playing. It's amazing how music soothes me. It always has.

"Hey, that sounds good," Dad says when he finally emerges in a black and red bathrobe, his hair sticking straight up.

"Thanks." I set my guitar aside. "Rough night?"

He rubs his stubbly chin and chuckles. "Not particularly."

I want to mention that he got home kind of late but control myself. He asks about the game and I tell him a little. I consider mentioning Harris to him, but my mom has trained me well. Best to keep my mouth shut about boys. Pretend I don't even know they exist. And while Dad is way more laid-back than Mom, I'm still not willing to risk this. However, I do decide to mention the guitar lessons.

"Really?" He takes a sip of coffee. "You're that good?"

I shrug. "I don't know. But this guy wants to learn and I offered to help him."

"That's nice." Now his brows lift. "Is he a good-looking guy?"

I roll my eyes. "Oh, Dad."

He laughs. "Just curious."

"I guess so." I look around the living room. "I thought about giving the lessons here, but I don't want to disturb you or—"

"Not a problem. Estelle wanted to drive over to Monterey today. I thought you might want to come, but if you have other plans . . ."

"I did promise to do the lesson," I say, trying not to look too eager.

Dad tilts his head to the side. "Okay, if you don't mind."

"Not at all. How far away is Monterey anyway?"

"About two and a half hours if the traffic's good."

"Oh . . . that's a lot of driving."

He nods. "But she really wants to go and I've been promising her for a while now."

"So you'll probably be home late again?"

He shrugs like he's unsure, but I can tell by his expression that he knows they'll be late and that he's a little uncomfortable about it.

"It's not a problem. I just wondered."

He smiles. "You're a good kid, Haley."

"You're a good dad, Dad."

"Well, I better grab a shower. Estelle will be here in about twenty minutes. She's insisting on driving."

"That's nice for you."

He nods. "Yeah. She's got a Mustang convertible that's a nice little ride."

"Sounds like fun."

He pauses as he's going into the hallway. "You're sure you don't want to come along?"

"Positive. In fact, I have some homework I should probably work on today."

"Okay. And maybe we can do something together tomorrow."

"Great." I smile.

As Dad is getting ready for his day trip with Estelle, I start to worry about whether or not Estelle's little brother will report to her that he saw me kissing Harris in Wet Willie's parking lot. I can't see any reason Buck would do that, but who knows? Then again, Estelle seems pretty cool about that sort of thing. And it doesn't take a genius to figure out why Dad came home so late last night. So hopefully she's into the whole live-and-let-live thing too. Besides, there's no law against kissing.

Estelle arrives at just a little past noon. "You look pretty," I tell her as I let her into the condo. She's wearing white pants and a yellow sweater set—very classic and mature looking compared to last weekend. Is she trying to look older for Dad's sake?

"Thanks." She pats her sleek blonde hair. "Although, I'll probably look totally frazzled before the day is over. Your dad likes us driving with the top down. You coming, Gordon?" she yells down the hallway.

Before long, Dad's ready and they both tell me good-bye and to have a good day, and, once again, I have the condo all to myself. Only this time, instead of feeling a little left out and lonely, I'm totally jazzed. I can have Harris over here and not worry about a thing.

I go around straightening things up, making the place appear as tidy as a bachelor pad can possibly look—I even dust the ficus plant—and then I check my phone again. Still no calls, no texts. Has he forgotten me?

Harris doesn't call until after three and I try not to sound impatient or overly eager, but it's not easy.

"So is now a good time to come over there?" he asks hopefully.

"Sure." Then I explain how my dad and his girlfriend have gone to Monterey for the day.

"Cool, I'll be there in about fifteen, okay?"

"Okay." I close my phone, then rush to the bathroom to: (1) brush my teeth, (2) check my hair, and (3) put on some fresh lip gloss. Then I open the door to the terrace since the sun has come out and I sit out there playing my guitar until I hear the doorbell ringing. Suppressing my nerves and trying to act very casual, I open it.

"Come on in," I tell him as he carries his guitar case into the living room and looks around.

"This is a cool little place." He sits on the black leather sofa. "Very manly."

I laugh and sit down in one of the chairs. "Yeah, I noticed."

Harris pats the seat of the sofa next to him. "Why are you so far away?"

I giggle, then go over and sit down, but as soon as I do this, I wish I hadn't. I don't want to look too eager . . . too easy. But then just like last night, we are kissing again. It feels a little different in the bright light of day and at first I feel self-conscious, but before long I'm used to it. Then after a while, just like last night, Harris's hands are wandering again. And suddenly I feel like I need to draw some boundaries—without offending him.

I sit up and shake my head. "Harris, this is supposed to be a guitar lesson, remember?"

He looks disappointed.

"Or was that just a line?" I frown. "I thought you really wanted to learn guitar."

He gives a sheepish smile. "I do. But I guess that's not all I want."

I laugh and go get my guitar. "Come on. Let's do this right, okay? Playing guitar is really fun and I'd love it if we could play together."

Now he brightens. "That'd be cool."

So for the next couple of hours, we work on the basic chords and some simple picking and strumming techniques, and we actually manage to play a song together. Harris seems quite pleased with himself. "That was great," I tell him.

"You're a good teacher." He zips his soft guitar case closed.

"Thanks!" But now he pats the spot next to him on the sofa again and I know exactly where this is going.

Instead of joining him, I tilt my head to one side and study him, almost wishing he wasn't so good-looking. It would be very easy to go over there and comply with his wishes and kiss some more. But I'm starting to get worried. The more we kiss, the more he seems to want to push things further — further than I thought I wanted to go.

I consider mentioning this to him, but I'm not even sure how to put it. How do you tell the guy you love that you're not ready to have sex with him? What if he dumps you?

"Okay, okay . . . I get it." He stands and I'm worried he's going to leave and never speak to me again.

"Get what?"

"I promised you a real date, and that's what you're waiting for, right?"

I glance at the wall clock in the dining room, then nod. "Well, it's almost six now. I suppose if we were going to go on a real date, I might want a chance to get ready."

He looks down at his sports shorts and flip-flops. "Me, too. How about I come back and get you at about a quarter to seven? Can you be ready that fast?"

"No problem."

Now he looks at the clock. "By the way, when does your dad get home? Do you need to check with him first?"

"He said he'll be home late, but it's okay if I go out. Dad and I kind of have an understanding. He goes his way and I go mine. We're very adult." I giggle.

"Nice arrangement." Harris nods. "Wish my parents were more like that. I mean, here I am almost eighteen, going to college next year, and they still treat me like a juvenile sometimes."

"My mom was like that—and more so. I don't miss it at all."

"I'll bet you don't." Now we kiss good-bye, and for some reason I get the feeling that I have more power in this relationship than I thought before. I just need to remember to use it, draw the line, assert myself. Even if you love someone, you don't have to let them push you around.

I'm sure I'll eventually need to figure out a way to let Harris know I'm not ready for sex. Although I'm surprised I'm partly questioning my abstinence pledge now—a part of me wonders . . . I mean, if I'm in a committed and loving relationship (kind of like Dad and Estelle), then is it okay?

Yet at the same time, another part of me firmly says *no*, do not compromise, do not give in—stick to your guns and

···[CHAPTER 8]················

I honestly don't think it will matter where Harris takes me tonight. A taco stand or McDonald's or peanut butter and jelly sandwiches in his car would be just fine—as long as we are together. Plus, with so many butterflies in my stomach, I wonder if I can even eat at all. Even if this is my second date, it feels like a first and I'm so nervous I feel giddy. I hope I don't say anything too stupid.

"If we do something quick for dinner, there's a movie we can catch at seven thirty." Harris starts his car. "That is, if you like action flicks. Do you?"

"Sure," I tell him. Okay, that's not exactly honest. In fact, it's a great big lie. But I feel like I can make it true. Because if I'm watching an action movie with Harris, I will love it. I know I will.

"Great. I've really wanted to see it. A lot of girls aren't into that kind of thing, but I had a feeling you'd be more open-minded."

"I try to be open-minded. I really don't like being around people with closed minds. It seems to lead directly to bigotry and smallness."

He nods, then points toward the strip where several fast-food restaurants are located. "You have any preferences?"

"What's your favorite?"

He shrugs. "I kinda like the fish and chips place, but if you're like other girls, you probably think it's too greasy."

I laugh. "I love fish and chips."

"Really?" He grins at me. "See, I knew you were my kind of girl!"

Thankfully, I wasn't lying this time—I really do love fish and chips. And although I don't order the same size basket as Harris, I don't get the smallest one either. After a few minutes we are settled at a tiny wooden table, so close that our knees are touching and it feels like little sparks of electricity are flowing between us.

"Do you like malt vinegar on yours?" Harris asks me.

I really don't, but because he's generously pouring that brown stuff on his, I tell him I do. He hands me the bottle and I follow his lead by dousing my food, and the fumes coming up from the vinegar make my eyes water. I blink and take a bite, bracing myself for the bitterness and managing to keep a pleasant expression on my face.

I wish I hadn't done that—and I don't even know why I did. It's like I'm in second grade again, trying to be just like my new best friend. But how desperate and pathetic is that? Still, it's like I can't control myself. I so badly want this relationship to work and to last.

"Have you always loved football?" I reach for my soda, longing for something sweet to wipe out the bitterness.

"I guess. My dad is really into it. He started me playing when I was really little. And he still has the crazy idea that I can get a football scholarship."

"Can you?"

He shakes his head. "I doubt it. You have to be really good."

"But you are really good." I look into his eyes. "I was amazed at how good you are, Harris."

He chuckles. "Thanks. But we're in a relatively small league. I just don't think it measures up to some of the bigger ones."

"Would you even want to play college football?"

He shrugs. "I don't know."

"It seems like it can get dangerous."

"It's pretty dangerous now. You hadn't moved here yet, but early in the season a quarterback from our rival, Preston High, suffered a really nasty neck injury. He could've been a quadriplegic, but I heard he's getting his hands back. Although he still hasn't recovered the use of his legs, maybe never will."

"That's terrible."

"You're telling me."

"Do you like other sports?"

"I like baseball. And I used to play soccer, but Dad thought it was a wuss sport."

I laugh. "I used to play soccer too. And I was on swim team for a while. I actually really liked that."

"I noticed a pool at your condo."

"Yeah, I've been swimming some laps."

His brows lift. "I'd like to see that."

"Me swimming laps?"

"You in a swimsuit."

I smirk at him. "Well, you'd probably be disappointed since I wear my old team suit to swim laps."

"Hey, I happen to think those team suits are pretty sexy."

My cheeks grow warmer, but I just shake my head.

"Is your pool open at night?"

"Sure."

"Maybe we should take a dip after the movie."

I shrug. "I guess we could. But did you bring a suit?"

"No, but my neighborhood's not far from your condo. I could run and get it, and then we could have a moonlight swim."

I'm not sure how comfortable I am with this, but there's no way I'm going to tell him no. "Why not?" I say as I look for a fry not drowning in vinegar.

"Maybe we can do some racing. I'm not such a bad swimmer either."

"You're on. But keep in mind I can be pretty competitive. You won't hate me if I beat you, will you?"

He laughs. "You are my kind of girl."

After fish and chips, we make it to the movie in time to get popcorn and drinks, which is a relief since I still have the taste of vinegar in my mouth. With the movie trailers playing, Harris navigates us to a row near the front. "I like to really experience it up close and personal," he quietly tells me as we slip into our seats.

Before long our movie starts and, no surprises, it is loud and violent and full of swearing. My mother would've walked out on it in the first thirty seconds. Well, she never would've come in the first place since "movies are the Devil's work." But she would flip out if she knew I was here, and seeing Harris's hand fondling my bare knee would probably give the poor woman a heart attack. But I don't want to think about that.

Sometimes, when a scene is too brutal or bloody, I just close my eyes. Hopefully Harris won't notice. As much as I want to like the things he likes, I suspect I will never truly enjoy movies like this. They make me feel sick inside and I wonder how it's possible that people (guys mostly) love them. My favorite movie (and I'll probably never tell Harris this) is *The Sound of Music*. I know it's hokey and old-fashioned, but I still love it. There's an old VHS tape of it at my mom's, and I used to sneak it out and watch it when she wasn't around.

It wasn't that Mom disliked that movie, but I just wanted to enjoy it without her negative commentary or cynical remarks. My favorite scene, of late, is Liesl and Rolfe dancing in the gazebo after it started to rain. It is so romantic. Too bad Rolfe turned out to be such a jerk. Sometimes I like to imagine that he changed and accepted the captain's offer and escaped across the mountains with the Von Trapps and eventually married Liesl. But I suppose that makes me a hopeless romantic.

Finally the boom-boom-shoot-'em-up movie comes to a loud and destructive end, and I'm so relieved I clap enthusiastically with the others. All the way to the condo, Harris talks about the movie and the special effects and speculates on what the sequel will be like.

"I'll drop you off," he tells me as he pulls into the parking lot, "then run home and get my suit."

"Okay." I had actually hoped I'd get to ride with him to his house so I could see where he lives.

"About fifteen minutes, okay? Want to meet at the pool?"

"Sounds good." I wave good-bye, then head up to change into my suit. I wish I had a better-looking suit to wear. My old team suit is not only fairly worn but pretty snug, too. Still, Harris said he likes team suits and it's not like I have much choice in the matter.

I get into my suit and grab a couple of towels just in case he forgets. Then with my key in hand, I traipse on down to the pool. Because the night air is a little chilly and the water feels warm in comparison, I slip into the pool and start swimming laps. I love how the silky feel of the water relaxes me and I'm glad I shaved my legs this morning. I'm just finishing my fourth lap when I see Harris, fully dressed, standing outside the pool gate. I run and let him in.

"Where's your suit?"

He starts undoing his jeans. "I'm wearing it."

Soon we're both in the water and I challenge him to our first race. He's fast but I win. "Go again," he tells me eagerly. So we do and this time he beats me by a stroke.

"Ha!" he says victoriously, reaching over and pulling me to him. "To the victor go the spoils."

I frown. "I'm the spoils?"

His face is close to mine. "No, but you could spoil me if you wanted." And now we are kissing and our kisses are wet and slippery and exciting. He pulls me even closer and my heart is racing as I feel his skin against mine. His breath and his kisses—they're intoxicating. I enjoy it for a while, but then it's getting carried away—and who knows who might be watching.

"We're tied now," I breathlessly tell him. "Want to go best two out of three?"

"Again?" He looks disappointed, but I'm already against the wall ready to race.

"Come on, or are you chicken?"

He laughs and comes over beside me. "You asked for it."

"On your mark, get set, go!" I yell and we both streak across the pool and back, side by side the whole time.

"I won!" he proclaims.

"It was a tie," I shoot back.

"My hand hit the side first."

I make a face. "I want to see the digital playback."

He laughs and pulls me to him again. "I clearly won and now you owe me a prize."

"What kind of prize?" But already he's kissing me again. We kiss and kiss, both above and beneath the water, and he holds me so close, with our legs entangled, that I almost feel like we're one entity, some kind of weird octopus with four arms and four legs.

"Is your dad home yet?" he whispers in my ear.

This sends a start through me. He wasn't home when I changed into my suit, but what if he is now? I push Harris away and look up at our unit, trying to see if there's anyone looking down this way from the darkened terrace. But the lights around the pool and the chlorine in my eyes make it hard to see.

"I don't know. He wasn't home earlier."

"Want to go up and check?" Harris asks hopefully. "I'm starting to get cold and it would be nice to dry off some before I go home."

"Yeah." I nod. "I'll go check." I climb out of the pool and grab a towel, wrapping it around me like a sarong. "There's a towel for you," I call out as I leave.

I feel nervous as I go up the stairs. What if Dad is home? What if he's been watching us? What will he say? More important, what will I say? To my huge relief, Dad isn't home yet. So I go out to the terrace, turn on the light, and quietly call down to the pool. "The coast is clear."

Harris climbs out and gets his towel. "Thanks," he tells me as I let him in. "I was starting to feel like an ice cube down there."

"You use the bathroom. I'll change in my bedroom."

We go our separate ways and I hurry into some warm-ups and attempt to towel dry and brush out my hair. I'm just putting on some lip gloss when I hear Harris. "You coming out of there or should I come in and get—"

"Here I am," I say as I emerge from my room.

He grins suggestively and pulls me toward him. "I wouldn't have minded coming in there to get you."

I make a forced laugh. "Yes, I'm sure you wouldn't have." It's becoming pretty obvious that this guy is way more experienced than I am. For that matter, I'm positive that most of the U.S. teen population is way more experienced than I am. Not that I plan to reveal this to anyone.

Harris makes small talk as he guides me into the living room, where the lights are dimmed. We sit on the sofa and he slips his arm around me. "This has been a great night, Haley. I had no idea you were this much fun."

I feel a ripple of delight over this praise. "I've had fun too, Harris, even if you did cheat at swimming."

"I didn't cheat." He tickles me around my waist. "I won fair and square, admit it."

"No," I shriek with laughter, "you cheated!"

Now we're having a wrestling match, which goes from the couch to the floor. We're both laughing and teasing and then suddenly he is straddling me, pinning both my arms to the floor over my head. If he wasn't grinning, I might be scared. I had no idea he was so strong. "Admit it, Haley, I won."

Between giggles, I admit that he may have won. Then he leans down, landing a passionate kiss on me, then another. I feel like I'm being swept away by this, like being pulled out with the tide, like I want to just drown in his affection. But then I hear something at the front door.

"My dad!" I hiss at him. "He's home!"

In the same instant Harris jumps off me, straightens his clothes and hair, flips on the lights, reaches for the remote, and flops down onto the sofa. I try to follow his lead but am slower and just barely on my feet when my dad steps into the house.

"Hey, Dad," I say in way too sweet a voice, "you're home."
I walk past him and into the kitchen, where I dig in the fridge
for a couple of sodas, like this was what I was doing. "Harris is
here," I call over my shoulder. "I'd like you to meet him." I feel
rather pleased with how well I'm handling this, very grown-up,
I think.

Dad goes into the living room and I introduce them, and to
my relief Harris steps right in, telling Dad about the movie we
saw tonight and how we took a swim afterward, going into
detail of how he beat me in our swim race. "Although Haley is
really fast for a girl."

"She used to be on swim team." Dad hangs up his jacket.
Then I ask Dad about Monterey and he briefly describes their
day.

"Sounds like a good time." Harris is standing now. "Speaking
of time, I should get going. I have an eleven o'clock curfew."

I walk him outside, where we exchange one last good-night
kiss. "That ended too soon," he says wistfully.

"I know," I whisper back.

He smiles. "Until next time."

I watch as he goes down the stairs, almost feeling that my
heart is going with him. I stand there for a few minutes, trying
to take this all in. Talk about a whirlwind romance; that is
exactly what this feels like. I love him, love him, love him — and
I really don't want to lose him. Still, as I go back inside, I feel
nervous about how quickly things are moving. I know I'm in
way over my head right now, but I'm just hoping I can figure it
all out as I go along.

CHAPTER 9

n Sunday morning, Dad insists that he and I do something together. Somehow he's gotten the idea that I'm put out with him for spending the whole day with Estelle yesterday. He couldn't be more wrong. Still, I try to play along as we eat our cold cereal.

"So what do you want to do?" he asks for about the thirteenth time.

"Like I said, I don't really know. What do you usually do on Sundays?"

"I usually do something with Estelle."

"Then maybe you should—"

"We've already been through that. I told Estelle that today was for you."

"Was she mad?"

He shrugs, then refills his coffee mug.

"She wasn't happy, was she?"

"Estelle likes to have fun on the weekends. She works hard all week and figures the weekend should make up for it."

"Can't blame her for that."

"But back to us and today." Dad sets his mug firmly on the countertop. "Tell me what you'd like to do."

If I told Dad what I really wanted to do, he'd be hurt. What I really want to do is spend the day with Harris.

"You seemed to enjoy shopping last weekend. I suppose we could do something like that again."

I frown. "You really think your credit card can afford it?"

He laughs. "I think so."

I consider this. If we go shopping, we'll still be within cell phone range, whereas if we go out into the "wilderness" to hike and take photos like he suggested earlier, we might not be. Also it would take longer to get there and back. And I'm really hoping Harris wants to do something before the day is over.

"Sure," I tell Dad. "Shopping is fine. But maybe we should invite Estelle to come along."

Dad looks surprised. "Really? You want her to come?"

"Why not? She's a fantastic shopper and she's fun." Okay, that might be overstating it, but it's for Dad.

He looks like I just handed him a thousand dollar bill. "So you like her then?"

"Yeah, I like her. What did you think?" Okay, here I go lying again. I do not particularly like Estelle. In fact, I sort of dislike her a lot. But I do like that she occupies Dad and that frees me up a lot. I've decided that Estelle is a very handy woman to have around. Although I feel like a real hypocrite for think- ing that.

"I just didn't get the impression you were that fond of her." Dad reaches for the phone. "I'm actually really relieved to hear this, Haley."

I make what feels like a phony smile. "Tell her hey for me. I'll go get ready."

Back in my room I stare at myself in the mirror. Who am I? Who am I becoming? But then I think of Harris and decide

I don't really care. What matters most is keeping him. I want to keep him . . . maybe forever.

To that purpose I go shopping with Dad and Estelle again. Oh, Dad pulls his "I gotta check my e-mail and the stocks" routine again. But everyone seems happy and I actually score some new clothes out of the deal. Now that Harris is in my life, clothes seem more important than they did last week. And Estelle is great at finding the kinds of things that make me look hot and really show off my figure, which she keeps pointing out is "totally fabulous."

So maybe I like Estelle after all. Mostly I'm relieved that her "little" brother (aka Uncle Buck) isn't ratting on me for making out with Harris in the Wet Willie's parking lot on Friday night. Somehow I know that wouldn't sound good to my dad. And as it is, he seems to like Harris. I'd like to keep it that way. Perhaps I can keep it that way for years to come . . . because I truly think Harris and I are the real thing. I would never admit this to anyone (because it sounds so corny), but I want to marry that boy. I really, really do!

· · · · · · · · · · ·

My communication with Harris is minimal on Sunday, but at least he's in touch and texts me that he got roped into some family function. I text him back saying I'm doing the same. Then he says he'll call me later tonight.

So after dinner I go to my room on the pretense of homework, but keeping my phone at my elbow, I'm really surfing the Net and listening to music. It's almost nine when my phone rings.

"I've missed you," he says first thing.

"I missed you too."

We talk about our day a bit, then we talk about each other—how much we like each other, how cool it is we're together. Finally he says he needs to go and offers me a ride to school.

"Sounds good," I say, although I want to jump up and down and squeal. He says what time, then we say a gushy good night, and I close my phone and fall onto my bed. He's still into me! I am so happy. And I can't believe I'm now one of those girls who gets to ride with her boyfriend to school. Life is good. I carefully lay out what I want to wear tomorrow. Thanks to today's shopping spree, my closet is looking more like a real closet—and I feel like a real teenage girl. Not like the nun my mother was trying to force me to be.

On Monday morning, I head down to the parking lot at the time Harris told me. I could wait to see if he comes up to get me, but it's really no trouble to go down there. He's a few minutes late and seems surprised that I'm waiting for him.

"Sorry I'm late." He pulls into the street. "But you could've waited in the house. I would've called you."

"Oh." I nod. I probably looked overeager by standing in the parking lot. "I just wanted some fresh air."

"Yeah, it's a nice day all right."

We make small talk as he drives, but at the stop sign, his hand wanders over and he gives my thigh a squeeze. "I missed you, Haley."

I smile. "Me, too."

At school he comes around and opens my door, helps me out, and then pulls me into his arms. "I really missed you," he says passionately. Now we kiss and I feel myself melting again. Part of me wants to glance around to see if anyone is looking. Another part of me doesn't care in the least.

"We better get to class," I finally tell him as I pull away.

"Yeah." His voice sounds husky. "I guess so."

We hold hands as we walk into school, and I try to keep a perfectly natural expression on my face. I want to act like this is no big deal, like I've had lots of boyfriends and Harris is just one more. But underneath my cool veneer, I am trembling with excitement. This is so cool.

I can feel people looking at us. Some with mild interest. Others, like Emery's friends, openly stare. A few say hey and we greet them back. Harris seems a little nervous too. But he walks me all the way to my locker and plants another kiss on my lips. "See ya later, Haley."

I open my locker, resisting the urge to stick my head inside and giggle with glee, and I remove what I need, then close it. When I turn around, Emery is looking at me. It's not a mean look exactly. More like she's curious or confused. I attempt a weak smile in her direction. She seems to take that as an invitation and comes over.

"I'm not blaming you for the breakup," she tells me evenly. "Everyone knows it was just a matter of time with Harris and me." She looks around, as if wanting to see if anyone else is listening. "But just so you know, I will get him back . . . eventually."

My brows arch but I try not to look alarmed. "I guess we'll see about that."

She nods. "We most definitely will."

Now I force a bigger smile. "I'm just glad you're not mad at me. I really didn't want to make any enemies."

She smiles back and I'm surprised at how truly pretty she is—strikingly pretty. "No, I don't like to make enemies either. At least we agree on that." She turns and walks away, holding her head high. Her confidence shakes me, but I try to act like I'm unaffected, like I don't feel like a peasant in front of the queen.

Don't be ridiculous, I chide myself. Emery isn't superior to me or anyone. It's just that she acts like she is — oh, in a sugar-coated, friendly way — but it's not like I have to buy into it. Besides, I have Harris.

Lunchtime is a little precarious. I've decided to remain low-key, hoping I can stay beneath Saundra's and some of the others' radar. I wait for Harris to come into the cafeteria, then follow his lead as we get our food and go to the regular table.

"Oh, look, here comes the happy couple," someone says.

Now we get some teasing tossed our way. Some good-natured jabs, some with sharper barbs attached. But after a while they seem to grow bored and start talking about last week's game and how this week's is even more important.

"Having a new girlfriend better not slow you down," one of the guys says to Harris.

"Don't worry." Harris gently elbows me. "This girl is keeping me in shape." He chuckles like this is a private joke, so I laugh too.

This evokes some off-color comments and jokes, and my cheeks burn. I can also feel Emery's eyes on me. I know what's going on too — I may be naive, but I'm not stupid. Everyone here is assuming Harris and I have had sex. Part of me thinks I should just go along with this charade, but another part of me wants to raise my hand and make a statement of innocence. Naturally, I listen to the first part.

Somehow I make it through lunch with a smidgeon of dignity attached. Harris walks me to class and kisses me, and I think maybe I can keep up this charade after all.

"So you've gone ahead and done it," Poppie says to me in art class.

"Done what?"

"Gone all the way over to the dark side."

"Huh?" I select a very thin watercolor brush, then give her a blank look.

"You and Harris Stephens, you're a couple now."

"Oh." I just shrug, heading back to the worktable. "Is there a law against that?"

"Not if you want to ruin your life."

I turn and stare at her. "Ruin my life? Don't you think that's being a little melodramatic?"

She makes an uneasy smile as she sits down. "Maybe so. But I've heard things about Harris, how he rolls. I just didn't think you were like that, Haley."

"Me neither," Zach says as he joins us at the table.

"It's touching that you two are so interested in my private affairs." I sit down too. "But I really think you should get a life of your own."

"Ooh." Zach pulls his head back like I just zapped him. "Ouch."

"Excuse us for caring about you," Poppie says.

"I think it's sweet that you care," I tell her. "But I just don't get why you're so worried. Harris is a great guy. We had a wonderful weekend and—"

"Really?" Zach leans forward with way too much interest. "What did you and Harris do this weekend?"

"None of your business," I sweetly tell him.

"Aw." He makes a face.

"Well, I just hope you know what you're getting into." Poppie dips her brush in water, then turns her focus onto her painting of an old building.

"What she said." Zach's expression gets serious. "Watch out."

I roll my eyes, then divert my attention to my own piece. I'm painting an old rusty pickup parked in the middle of a field, with crows sitting on it. I found the picture in a magazine and for some reason liked it. Maybe I'll mat and frame it and give it to Harris when it's finished.

After school Harris meets me in the hallway. "I have practice, you know," he tells me, "but I'll call you after, okay?"

"Okay."

He leans in and kisses me, long and passionately, and I wish he didn't have to go to practice. But I just smile and tell him, "Later." As I walk to my locker, I feel like I'm walking on clouds. I'm beginning to understand all the clichés people use to describe love. It's like I've finally been allowed into this secret universe — and I like it here.

When I open my locker, a folded piece of white paper slides out. I bend to pick it up, thinking it's an assignment sheet that slipped out of my notebook, but it's actually a note — to me. It's not handwritten but printed in just a regular font, and glancing to the bottom, I see it's unsigned. Apparently whoever wrote it wants to remain anonymous. Sensing someone (maybe even the writer of this note) is watching me, I shove it into my bag, grab what I need, then close my locker. When I turn around, I just see the usual people milling about. I sling the strap of my bag over my shoulder, then holding my head high, like I've seen Emery do, I walk down the hallway and exit the school.

I don't mind walking home from school, and really it's much better than the bus. The condo's not far from school, and as long as the weather is like today, it's actually quite pleasant. Besides, it helps me clear my head. Maybe someday I'll even hang out and watch football practice, although I don't want to look like a groupie. But it could be fun.

However, at the moment, all I want to do is read the contents of that mysterious letter. I would've read it at school except I'm worried it's a hate letter — maybe written by an Emery fan. I didn't want to give anyone the pleasure of seeing me get undone by their words. I'm tempted to pull it out right here on the street, but I really want to read it in the privacy of my own home. So I pick up the pace.

Finally I'm inside the condo, digging through my bag for the letter. I unfold it and begin to read.

Dear Haley,

I probably shouldn't be writing this to you, but I am. I know you're new here and you don't know everyone in school — not the way I do. So I want to give you a friendly word of warning. You seem like a nice girl and you probably have no idea that Harris Stephens is dangerous. Very dangerous. I'm warning you to watch out and, if you're smart, I'm advising you to break up with him. The sooner the better. Believe me, if you don't you will be sorry. Very sorry. I hope you will take this warning seriously. Those who play with fire will get burned — and you will be no different. Lose him while you can.

Sincerely,
X

I'm not sure what a poison-pen letter is, but this one feels toxic to me. What kind of lowlife would write something like this? It's so creepy; I don't even want to touch it. And I'm determined to destroy it. But I decide to read it once more just to see if I can guess who wrote it and why. I read it again, more slowly, and try to imagine someone like Emery or one of her close friends writing something like this, but it just seems weird.

Still, I do remember the determined look in Emery's eyes when she told me she'd get Harris back. Perhaps she'd stoop to writing a threatening letter. That's what this feels like. Oh, the writer can call it a warning, like she cares about me, but it's really a fear tactic. Someone wants to scare me away from Harris. Probably so Emery can have him back.

Well, what she doesn't know is that I don't scare that easily. She also doesn't know how much I love Harris. To think a silly letter like this would change that is ridiculous.

I find some matches, take the letter to my bathroom, and burn it in the sink, washing the ashes down. I need to forget the whole thing. Stupid letters like that should've been over and done with in middle school. Someone needs to grow up!

When Harris calls me later that night, I consider telling him about it but decide not to. Why worry him with some crazed person's rant? Besides, I just want to wash the whole thing away. No sense in letting a dumb letter spoil what Harris and I have found in each other.

"I can't wait to go out with you again," Harris tells me as we're trying to say good night and hang up.

"Me, too," I murmur.

"Well, Friday, as you know, is a game night and we can't go out after that because I have to go with my parents to San Francisco because my brother is getting married on Saturday morning and my mom wants to get there the night before."

"You have a brother who's getting married?" I feel surprised not to know this.

"Yeah. Leo is almost ten years older than me. His girlfriend, Julie, finally got him to tie the knot. And I'm even supposed to be in the wedding."

"Sounds like fun."

"Maybe to you. I'm not too thrilled to put on a monkey suit and escort strangers down the aisle."

"You'll look handsome in a tux. Will you send me a photo?"

"I'll try. Anyway, I think we'll get home in time for a date Saturday night, if you're interested."

"Sure, I'd like that."

"I want it to be a special date, Haley."

I feel a warm rush. "Sounds good to me."

"Cool. I just thought I'd get it all set so we can look forward to it this week."

"I'm already looking forward to it."

"Me, too." He lets out a loud sigh. "Someday, when football season is over, we'll have more time to be together. Until then, we'll just have to squeeze in what we can." He chuckles. "Wish I could squeeze a little something right now."

I laugh. "I should probably get back to my homework." Which is the truth. Already I feel like I'm falling behind. I think it's because I've been distracted. Or else you lose some brain cells when you're in love. Or maybe it's a combination of both.

It's true what they say — time really does fly when you're having fun. I can hardly believe a whole week has passed since Harris and I have been a couple. It seems like a few moments or maybe a day, but not a week.

Even the Friday night football game goes by too quickly. It's an away game and I manage to snag a ride with Libby, and throughout the game I keep my eyes on Harris and a couple of times I actually pray that he doesn't get hurt. I can't believe I'm praying since I thought I gave that up, but I suppose love makes us do strange things.

Then, even though our team wins, I feel sad when the final buzzer goes off and the game is over. Oh, I don't show it. But knowing that Harris will be swept away by his parents as soon as he showers and changes from his uniform makes me blue. I want to be selfish with him.

"What's wrong with you?" Libby asks as her mom drives us to Wet Willie's.

"I'm fine."

"You're moping over Harris, aren't you?" she teases.

"No, I'm not. I understand that he needs to go to his brother's wedding. No big deal."

"Harris's brother is getting married?" Libby's mom asks.

"Yes," I tell her. "Tomorrow. In San Francisco."

She makes some parental comments about how just yesterday Leo was in diapers, and Libby and I exchange glances. I try to act cheerful at Wet Willie's and I remind myself I have a really great boyfriend who is taking me out tomorrow night, but it's not easy. I've never been a real social person, and without Harris to keep things going, I feel a little lost.

"What, no boyfriend to make out with in the parking lot?" Buck teases me as I'm going to the ladies' room.

I make a face at him. "Not tonight, Uncle Buck."

He laughs. "Well, I'm happy to step in for your missing man, Haley."

"Thanks anyway, but the idea of kissing Uncle Buck is more than a little disturbing." I can hear others laughing at this as I go into the restroom, and I think maybe I can learn to pull this off on my own. Still, I wish Harris were here.

When I come out of the stall, Emery is standing in front of the tiny mirror applying lip gloss. "Oh, hello," she says coolly. "I didn't know you were in here."

"Uh-huh." I keep my eyes down as I wash my hands.

"Harris is at Leo's wedding?"

I nod, then dry my hands.

"Yes, I was invited too."

I look up. "You were?"

She nods, slipping the tube of gloss into her bag. "Julie and I were good friends. In fact, she'll probably be disappointed I didn't go."

"Oh . . ."

"But under the circumstances, well, it didn't seem right."

"No, I suppose not."

"But I'm surprised Harris didn't take you." She's looking intently at me now, like she's trying to figure me out. "Or maybe you didn't want to go with him."

I toss the paper towel into the trash and just shrug. "Harris and I have only been together a week. It seems a little premature to be going to a wedding together, don't you think?"

She nods and smiles. "Yes, as a matter of fact, I do." Then she turns and leaves the restroom.

I don't know why this irritates me so much, but it does. It's like Emery is the prickly pin, always on hand to burst my happy bubble. But I won't let her. What Harris and I have, she cannot take away. I know it.

Still, after I'm home I wonder, did Emery write that mean letter? Is she trying to scare me away from Harris? It's obvious she wants him back. Why wouldn't she? But it just doesn't seem like her style to write an anonymous letter. I suspect if Emery had something to say, she'd say it (sweetly) right to my face. She'd be smiling and acting concerned for me when in reality she'd just be concerned for her image. Emery wouldn't want to risk her reputation as the nicest girl in school, not just one week before homecoming queen elections.

· · · · · · · · · ·

On Saturday, I don't feel much like doing anything. Dad even invites me to play racquetball with him, but I decline.

"Are you feeling okay?" he asks.

"Sure, I'm fine. But I do have some homework to catch up on."

"They sure pile it on these days — lots more than back when I was in school."

"Back in the dark ages," I tease.

He nods. "But a little fresh air and exercise is good for the brain, Haley. You sure I can't talk you into it?"

"Tempting, but I'll take a rain check." I'm fully aware that my lack of interest is due to only one thing. I feel like I'm on pins and needles waiting to hear from Harris, hoping he'll text me something about the wedding or send a photo—anything.

But the day slowly passes and I hear nothing. It's after five and I'm not sure if I should even get ready for our date or not. I'm sitting in the living room, flipping through the channels on TV, when Dad comes out neatly dressed.

"I'm taking Estelle to a play tonight." He adjusts his tie. "She's had tickets for weeks."

"Sounds nice." I force a smile.

"I'd invite you to join us except the thing is sold out." He chuckles. "I'd gladly let you go in my place, but Estelle would throw a fit."

"No, Dad. I don't want to go in your place. Besides, I think I have a date tonight."

"Really?" He looks relieved. "With Harris?"

I nod and smile.

"He seems like a very nice young man, Haley."

"He had to go to his brother's wedding this morning, over in San Francisco. Hopefully he'll get home in time to make our date."

Dad glances at his watch. "Well, the night's still young. But our play's in Fresno and I promised Estelle we'd have drinks first, so I better get moving."

"Have fun, Dad."

"You, too. And I expect it'll be another late night for me. We have reservations for a late dinner after the play."

"Well, then I won't wait up for you." I wink like this is a joke.

He laughs. "Good, I wouldn't expect you to."

Shortly after Dad leaves and to my huge relief, Harris calls. "We just got home, but I made a reservation for seven. Does that work for you?"

"Sounds great!" I am dancing around the living room as I say this. I can't believe he made a reservation. Not only is this a real date, it's a real date with a reservation.

"I'll be by a little before seven then, okay?"

"Perfect." As soon as I hang up, I start scrambling. I want to look absolutely perfect tonight, and I think I know exactly what I'll wear. Estelle talked me into getting a dress at the Gap and it really looks great on me. At first I balked because I'm just not a dress sort of girl. But she urged me to try on what she called "a little black dress," saying it was something every girl needed in her wardrobe.

I still didn't get why it was such a big deal — besides, the black dress looked kind of boring on the hanger. However, when I tried it on, I had to admit it looked pretty hot. Then when Estelle mentioned how guys like seeing a girl in a dress some-times, I was sold.

I take a shower and do my hair and makeup, then slip into the little black dress, which fits me perfectly, and look in the mirror. It's very sophisticated and sexy looking (in an under-stated and classic way), but the coolest part is that it makes me look older. Harris is almost eighteen, which sounds very grown-up, and I'm only sixteen, which sounds much younger. But to look like this — I do a spin to see the back of the dress — well, I could probably pass for twenty.

"Wow," Harris says when I open the door, letting him into the condo. "You look awesome, Haley."

"Thanks." I make what I think is a coquettish smile. It's something I've read about and means something like flirty. "You look nice too."

"It felt good to get out of that monkey suit," he says as we go down to the parking lot. "If I ever get married, it'll be on a beach somewhere and we won't even wear shoes."

My heart skips a beat over how he just said "*we* won't wear shoes," as if he's planning in the same direction as me. "A shoeless wedding sounds like fun. I think if I ever get married, I'd like to do it in Hawaii."

He nods. "Yeah, like Maui. I went there once with my family; it was great." As he drives, Harris tells me more about Maui. He talks about snorkeling and surfing and sailboats, and the whole while I am imagining a wonderful honeymoon with him on that romantic island.

He pulls into a steakhouse parking lot and I feel a little disappointed. This definitely would not be my first choice for a special date. But once we're inside, I realize it's a much more romantic place than I expected. White cloths on the tables, flickering candlelight, a fireplace, soft music. It's like something right out of an old movie and I love it.

"Great place," I tell him after we're seated.

"My parents used to love this place." He unfolds his linen napkin, setting it on his lap like someone trained him well. At first I suspect his mom . . . then I wonder about Emery. She has fairly impeccable manners. However, I'm not going there.

"What do you mean *used to*?" I follow his lead with my own napkin.

"They don't go out much anymore."

"Why not?"

He shrugs. "I think they're going through some marriage stuff."

I nod. "Oh . . . I know how that goes."

"I don't think they'll divorce or anything. But they don't seem to like each other as much as they used to. I guess that's what it's like to get old." He laughs.

I consider telling him that my dad and Estelle don't seem to have that problem, but talking about a parent's love life just feels like a downer, so I change the subject. "So how was the wedding and ushering little old ladies down the aisle?"

"It was okay." He takes a sip of water. "I never tripped or anything."

I chuckle. "I'm sure your brother was relieved."

"I think he was relieved just to get the whole thing over with." Now he goes on again about how silly formal weddings are. And although I don't agree with him on all of this (I've always dreamed of wearing a white lace dress and carrying delicate white rosebuds), I pretend that I understand his sentiments. Also, I imagine we're discussing our own wedding, which sends shivers of joy up and down my spine. I can't believe this is my life — sitting here with Harris, being in love . . . it's magical.

There's a lull in the conversation and I'm surprised no one has taken our order yet, but the place is pretty busy. Besides, why would I want to rush this evening when everything is absolutely perfect? "So how is your guitar playing coming along?" I ask. "Or have you been too busy to practice?"

"I've been practicing. Having that lesson with you makes me feel like I got over the hump, you know, the learning curve. Like I can sit down and work on stuff by myself now."

I frown. "Meaning you don't need any more lessons?"

He shakes his head. "No, not at all. I still have a lot to learn." He makes a mischievous grin. "And maybe you do too."

"About what?"

He just shrugs, and finally the waiter arrives and takes our drink orders. I go with my usual Coke and Harris orders the same. "I wish we were old enough to order something stronger," he tells me after the waiter leaves.

"Oh . . . ?" I try not to look too surprised.

He nods. "But I have something for later."

I divert my gaze to the menu. I'm trying not to react to this news, but I feel uncomfortable about it. I didn't realize Harris drank alcohol. I thought athletes got in trouble for that sort of thing. Don't they do some kind of testing? However, I try not to look flustered as I skim over the menu, trying to decide what to order.

Suddenly it occurs to me that the meals are not cheap here. Not like fish and chips. And I have no idea what kind of budget Harris might be on tonight. Most of his friends act like they're not too concerned with money, and I suspect their parents are fairly generous. But I'm not really sure about Harris's financial situation. He does have his own car—at least I think it's his—but, seriously, how does a girl know what to order?

"Is there anything you recommend?" I hope this isn't too obvious.

"All of their steaks are good."

"But are they huge?"

He considers this. "Yeah, they're pretty big. You might want something like the petite sirloin. My mom used to get that."

I nod. "Sounds good."

So when the waiter returns, I order the petite sirloin with a salad and Harris goes for a New York strip and the works. I am relieved—money must not be a big concern tonight.

"I feel like this is some kind of celebration," I say as I sip my soda.

"It is. We *are* celebrating."

"What are we celebrating?"

"Us." He holds up his soda glass. "Here's to us!"

"To us." I clink my glass against his.

Our dinner is served and I'm not sure if it's just me, but everything is absolutely perfect. If violins came and played at our table, I wouldn't even be a bit surprised. That doesn't happen but as we're splitting double Dutch chocolate cake for dessert, I feel myself getting lost in Harris's blue eyes. I truly can't imagine a better evening—and I have a good imagination!

After dinner Harris drives us to the city park, where we walk all the way around the small manmade lake. While watching the sun setting, I tell him about my favorite places in Oregon and he promises me we'll go there together someday. I feel like I'm truly in heaven. Really, how could a place in the clouds be any better than right here with Harris?

Finally it's too dark to see much and we get back into the car. "I brought my guitar," he tells me as he drives toward home. "I thought maybe I could come up to your place and we could play some more songs together."

"I . . . uh . . . I'm not sure," I say uncomfortably. I hadn't counted on this, and the last time I had Harris over, things got a little out of hand. "I, uh, I don't know exactly when my dad will be home." Okay, that's partially true.

"Does it matter?" He laughs. "I mean, I'm not really good yet, but my playing shouldn't hurt his ears too much."

Of course, that wasn't what I meant, but I laugh and say it doesn't matter. Then I tell him how it was my dad who originally got me hooked on the guitar. "He plays too. In fact, if he gets home while you're still there, we could have a little jam session."

"Cool."

Of course, when we get there, Dad is not home. I don't expect he'll be home before midnight. Maybe later. Harris seems fine with my absentee parent, and when he unzips his guitar case, he removes what looks like a bottle in a brown paper bag. "Can I mix you a drink?" he asks with a lopsided grin.

"I, uh, I don't know." I feel nervous now. How am I supposed to handle this? I know what my mother would say — something like "get thee behind me, Satan!" — but what do normal people do in this situation? I don't drink and I don't think minors should drink.

"Come on," he urges me. "I'll just make you a small drink so you can try it. You don't even have to drink it if you don't like it. *Okay?*"

I nod hesitantly. "Okay."

I go into the living room, nervously pacing. What would my dad say if he walked in right now? Would he be cool? Or would he turn into my mom? It's not likely I'll find out tonight.

"Here you go." Harris hands me what looks like an innocent glass of Coke on the rocks. *"Cheers!"*

"Cheers!" I take a cautious sip and am surprised that it doesn't taste much different than regular Coke. Sweeter and tangier and a little bit like medicine — a regular Coke would be better. But, really, this isn't too bad.

Harris and I sit down and play a few songs, and after a while he fills our glasses again. And eventually he stops playing and just listens to me as I finish up an old Beatles song, "Let It Be." While I'm playing, he comes over and starts massaging my neck . . . and then I realize he's kissing my neck . . . and soon I forget all about my guitar.

CHAPTER 11

I don't even remember how we got to my bedroom, but I'm aware we are here now. I'm also aware that the kissing has gotten way more passionate, and the touching and feeling has gone further than I dreamed possible—and I am not comfortable with this.

"That's enough now, Harris." I move his hand away and giggle as I hear the slur in my own voice. I sound like someone else.

He laughs too. "Never enough," he whispers in my ear. "I could never get enough of you, Haley. You are like my dream woman."

Dream woman? I do like the sound of that. Even so, I move his other hand away and attempt to sit up. "Lemme get up."

"Easy does it, girl." He pushes me back down on my bed. "What's the hurry?"

"I wanna get up." I try to sit up again.

"Not yet. We've barely gotten started here." This time he firmly pushes me with both hands.

"But, Harris—I wanna get up. Lemme up."

He uses one hand to hold me down on the bed. I'm surprised at how strong he is, surprised at the intense expression on his face, like he's someone else, not my sweet Harris. And then, with a rush of panic, I realize he's using his other hand to undo his belt.

"What're you doing?" I struggle to sit up again, but it's useless.

"Come on," he says in a husky voice, "you know you want me, Haley. You've been begging for this."

"No." Maybe it's adrenaline or just plain fear, but my head is starting to feel clearer. "No, I don't want to do—"

In the same instant he is on me—pinning me down with the weight of his body and his strength. My arms and legs are too weak. They feel like wet noodles against his power, but I keep telling him, *"No! No! No!"*

My heart and head pound as I keep trying to push him away from me, telling him again and again that I'm not ready for this, that he's got it all wrong, that I didn't ask for this. But he's not listening and he's getting rougher. What started out as a kissing session has turned into a real wrestling match, and I can tell he's enjoying it—and winning.

"Please, stop," I beg him. "I don't want this."

"I knew you were a tigress." He's huffing as he pushes and pulls at my dress. "I knew it would be like this. I've dreamed of this moment."

I struggle and fight and plead with him, but it's useless. Finally I experience a searing pain inside of me—like a knife slicing into me, cutting me in two—and I know it's too late. He has won.

I squeeze my eyes shut and bite my lip. Every muscle in my body is tense, stiff as a board as I wait for him to finish. Tears slide down my cheeks and I can taste salty blood in my mouth. I want to scream and cry out and even swear at him, but it's too late. Instead I bite harder into my lip, focusing on the pain in my mouth instead of the pain down inside of me. And finally, after what seems like an eternity, it's over. Harris lets out a loud sigh and rolls off me, breathing heavily but not saying a word.

I lie there, wondering what to do. I want to hit him and yell at him and throw him out of my room and my house. I want to kill him! But when I peek out of one eye at him, I'm shocked to see that he's sleeping peacefully. And he actually looks like his old self. How is that even possible?

I slide off my bed and grab my torn underwear from the floor, then tiptoe out of there and into the bathroom. Locking the door, I sit down on the floor and sob so loudly I think I'll wake Harris up. But I don't care. And I wouldn't even care if Dad came home right now. In fact, I *wish* he would come home. I would confess everything and tell him what Harris just did to me. And Dad could beat the stuffing out of Harris and I wouldn't protest a bit.

Thinking these thoughts only makes me cry louder. I am so lost. So confused. So messed up. It wasn't supposed to be like this. It's all wrong. Why couldn't I stop him? Why didn't he listen to me? I'm sobbing so loudly, I can't believe Harris can't hear me.

Eventually I feel a wet spot beneath me on the floor, and I assume I'm getting my period. I can't believe it — how is that even possible? How is any of this possible? Maybe it's a nightmare. I stand up and peer at my reflection in the mirror above the sink. My hair is ratty and mussed, I have black mascara streaks down my cheeks, and my lower lip is swollen and bloody. I am a mess. Worse than that, I feel like a mess. I feel soiled and betrayed . . . damaged.

I move the clothes hamper in front of the door like a barricade, then peel off my dress, noticing that it's torn in several places. I don't care — I hate this dress now. I wad it and my underwear into a ball and shove it into the cabinet beneath the sink, pushing it way back into a dark corner. Later I will burn it.

Then I get into the shower, turn the water on as hot as my body can stand, and scrub and scrub and scrub, washing myself until my skin is raw and red. When the hot water begins to turn cool, I turn off the tap and get out. The bathroom is so steamy, I can barely see. I find a towel and wrap it around me, then, still aching inside, I sit on the toilet seat and cry . . . and cry.

Why did this happen? How did this happen? I ask myself these questions again and again. Was it the alcohol? Did it change Harris into someone else? Or did I really send Harris the wrong signals? Or is he just like that, taking what he wants no matter what the other person says? I run all these questions and more through my head over and over, so many times that I feel dizzy and sick, like I just got off a bad carnival ride. And then I throw up.

For some reason I feel a little better after vomiting. I'm glad that the dinner Harris bought me and the drinks he fixed me are all being flushed down the toilet. I wish I could flush this whole night down the toilet too. If only . . .

I'm so tired that my whole body aches, and now I'm shivering, but I'm afraid to leave this bathroom, afraid to see Harris again, afraid of what I'll say . . . and even afraid of what he'll say. Will he try to make it seem like nothing happened, or will he think I'm a baby because I reacted so badly? What am I supposed to do with all this? And what if Dad comes home? I'm not sure I want him to beat up Harris now — what good would it do? And I certainly don't want to be discovered like this, hiding out in the bathroom with no clothes.

So, still wrapped in a towel, I quietly open the door. I listen intently, but hearing nothing, I creep to my bedroom door that is still partly opened. I peek inside my room and find that Harris is gone. His clothes and shoes are gone too. I go into my closet and pull on some warm-ups and consider staying there until morning, but after a while, I decide that's ridiculous.

So I tiptoe out to the living room to discover that his guitar is gone, as well as the bottle that contained the alcohol he poured into our drinks. Finding the front door unlocked, I realize Harris has let himself out. I quickly lock the door and clean up the glasses and all signs of what happened here tonight. Then I hurry back to my bedroom and climb into bed. It's almost two o'clock and I'm too tired to think, too tired to figure anything out. . . . All I want is to sleep . . . to escape this. I want to wake up in the morning to find out that it's all just a dream — a very disturbing dream.

· · · · · · · · · ·

I wake up early the next morning, and at first I can't fully remember what happened last night — then it hits me like a landslide. I'm buried beneath so many feelings I can't even sort them out, let alone understand them or deal with them.

With my heart pounding as hard as if I've just swum twenty laps, I start pacing in my room, bouncing back and forth between hostile rage and humiliating shame and everything in between. First I blame Harris . . . and then myself . . . and then my parents . . . and then I start all over again. I am so confused.

I feel desperate, like I need to figure this thing out, need to do something to fix it, need to make it go away. I think about Harris so hard my head hurts. Or maybe it's the drinks from last night that are making my head hurt. I go to my phone, checking to see if he's texted me. I'm not surprised to find he hasn't, but I am surprised at how devastated I am. Then I'm disgusted that I am so pathetic that I care enough to cry.

I slip down the hallway to the kitchen and pour myself a tall glass of orange juice, which I take back to my room and slowly drink. I can tell by Dad's keys on the table by the front door that he's home. Probably sleeping in. I want to take another long, hot shower but don't want to disturb Dad. Instead, I go down to the pool and swim laps.

The chilly water is shocking at first, but then it's soothing, and the coolness on my head makes the throbbing inside lighten up some. I swim and swim, trying to block out everything except the feeling of my arms and legs moving freely through the water, the sound of the water splashing, the smell of chlorine, and the rhythm of my breathing. Finally I'm so tired that my arms and legs feel like there are weights attached, and I drag myself out of the water and wrap up in my towel and just sit there in the morning sun. But it's not as warm out here as it looks and soon I'm shivering.

I go back inside where it's still quiet, and I take another steaming hot shower, scrubbing my skin so vigorously that I look like a boiled lobster when I finally step out. Like last night, the bathroom is so steamed up I can barely see. I dry off and go back to my room, climb into my bed, and fall asleep.

It's past noon when I wake up. The first thing I do is check my phone. Harris is still silent. I consider texting him but have no idea what to say. A part of me wants to lash out at him, call him names, demand to know why he did that. But another part of me wants to crawl back to him, say I'm sorry for making such a fuss, and ask him if he's picking me up for school tomorrow. Of course, I despise that part of me — that wimpy, pathetic girl who would lower herself to that place just to please a guy. What have I become?

Just the same, I resist the urge to send a message of any kind. My treatment for Harris will be silence. Let him wonder. Maybe he'll think about what he did and feel guilty. Maybe he'll apologize to me. Maybe he'll send me flowers.

When I leave my room, the house is quiet, and I can tell that Dad's been up and made coffee. Then I notice a note on the fridge, saying he's gone to meet Estelle for breakfast and to call him if I want to do anything with them today. Naturally, I don't call. I really don't want to see anyone today. I just want to hide out and hope things will get better. But how can they?

I wish, I wish, I wish . . . that I had someone to talk to. Someone to make sense of this mess I've made of my life, someone who could tell me what to do, how to clean this thing up. But I can think of no one. Mom would scorn me and say, "I told you so." My "best friend" from my other school (a friend from church) would be so disappointed in me that she'd probably sound just like my mom. My brother . . . well, he can't even sort out his own life. I wonder if Dad would understand, but I just cannot imagine telling him about what happened. He'd probably feel worried and guilty and confused, he'd wonder what had become of our "let's be grown-ups" pact, and he might even want to send me home to Mom.

Although when I consider going back home to Mom, I'm not nearly as opposed to it as I was before. In a way it would be a relief. Except for the way she would treat me. I don't think I could endure that. It's bad enough that I hate myself for what happened (and Harris, too) but to endure my mom's judgment, sermons, and restrictions on top of everything else . . . well, I don't think I can handle that much hatred.

As the afternoon wears on, I get extremely worried about facing Dad. What if he looks at me and knows? Every time I see myself in the mirror, it feels like everything that happened last night is written across my face. Besides the swollen bruised lip,

I can see it in my eyes, in the strained expression. How can I possibly hide all this pain? I make up a story about how I hurt my lip. While swimming laps this morning, I ran into the edge of the pool. I actually did that once and I think I can make it believable. As for the rest of me, I'll have to figure it out as I go.

I continue checking my phone off and on all day. Harris has not made a peep. I try to imagine what he's doing right now. Is he thinking about me? Does he have regret? Guilt? Fear? Would he be worried that I told my dad? What if my dad did something totally insane like calling the police? I've heard of cases like that. Although I honestly don't know what the police could do. After all, I invited Harris up here. I willingly engaged in underage drinking. I let him kiss me. I must've let him lead me to my room since I do not remember balking.

In all reality, I'm sure I would end up looking just as responsible for last night as Harris. Besides, how humiliating would it be to have to tell a stranger about everything, to answer personal questions . . . and then what if the whole thing became public? I would never want to show my face again. Even now, I'm not sure I can go to school tomorrow. Maybe I should just call my mom, confess everything, and take the punishment that will go with it.

When my phone rings midafternoon, I leap from where I've been vegging in front of the TV to get it. But it's not Harris. It's Dad.

"Estelle and I plan to catch a matinee. You want to come? We can swing by and get you."

"No thanks," I say brightly. "I've got homework."

"Okay. But remember what they say about all work and no play."

I force a laugh. "Don't worry, Dad. I'm not turning into a workaholic."

We make a little more small talk, but finally and to my relief, Dad says he better go. I let out a long sigh as I close my phone. Step one in tricking Dad into believing I'm perfectly fine. I pick up the remote and flip through the TV channels, searching for something—anything—to block out my thoughts . . . and the gnawing pain inside.

Finally I settle on a glitzy old movie from the sixties called *That Touch of Mink* that's just beginning. It stars Doris Day and Cary Grant, and in the beginning it seems like a sweet, simple story about a woman who falls in love with a very rich man. But as I watch, I realize it's really about a whole lot more, and as it progresses I can't believe it—Cary Grant's character expects Doris Day to have sex with him just because he bought her a bunch of stuff and took her on a trip. But she, like me, has been saving herself for marriage. It's touch and go there for a while, and sometimes I almost laugh, but eventually it ends happily when Cary Grant marries her.

I turn off the TV. What disturbs me most about this frothy movie was that Doris Day had a best friend. Throughout all her troubles, Doris had a roommate who watched out for her, warned her about men, listened to her, and tried to help.

And the reason I find this so upsetting is that I have no one like that in my life. No one! And it feels so unfair that I have to carry this burden on my own. I have never felt so totally alone in my entire life.

By Sunday night, I have assured Dad that nothing is wrong with me. I wouldn't have needed to do this except he asked me about last night's date and I almost started to cry.

"It's just that Harris and I had a little fight." And this wasn't entirely untrue. "You know how it goes sometimes. It's really no big deal."

"He seemed like such a nice guy." Dad looked disappointed. "Maybe you can patch things up."

"I . . . uh . . . I don't think so." I glanced away, not wanting to make eye contact. "I actually think we might break up. It might be for the best."

Again, this is probably not far from the truth. Especially considering that Harris has not texted or called or anything. I can think of no good excuse for his bad behavior except that he is over me. I just wish I were over him too.

The truth is, I still have feelings for him, and the more time passes, the more I start wondering about ways to smooth this whole thing over. I imagine myself going to him, saying that I'm sorry, that he caught me off guard, and that if he'll be a little more patient in the future, I will try to get with the program. I also consider pretending that my biggest concern is about birth control and that I have no intention of being sixteen and pregnant, but for all I know Harris might've used protection. I honestly can't remember anything past a certain point — besides pain, that is.

Of course, this sends me down a whole new road — *what if I am pregnant?* Why didn't I pay more attention to this stuff in health class last year? Probably because I mistakenly believed that my pledge of abstinence made me immune to such worries. So before going to bed, I go online and do some quick research, but by the time I finish reading several sites, I'm even more confused.

It's nearly midnight by the time I'm in bed. How would Harris feel if I was indeed pregnant — how would he deal with *that?* But I really don't want to think about this mess anymore. And I don't want to think about Harris. All I want to do is sleep this thing away. I may even attempt to play sick tomorrow and stay home from school. Maybe I'll be ill for an entire week. The comfort of thinking I could pull this off soothes me enough to fall asleep.

But tomorrow comes and I realize I can't afford to miss that much school. Also, call me crazy, but I'm hoping that Harris regrets his behavior Saturday night. Right now he might be rehearsing an apology for me. And after I dress, very carefully, I wait where I can see the parking lot and watch to see if his car is coming. Finally, it's just five minutes before school and I realize I need to walk . . . and that I'll be late.

I feel nervous as I go into the school building and past security. I am definitely late, which means I have to check in at the office and get a tardy slip to get into class. But it's a relief not seeing anyone I know in the halls — especially Harris. This gives me a chance to compose myself, and because I'm still considered a new student, the office assistant is fairly nice about the tardy slip.

As I go into my class, I keep my eyes downward, hand the teacher the note, and slip into a seat in back. It's impossible to focus on math and, fortunately, everyone is working quietly at their desks and I attempt to do likewise. At least I pretend that I am. But the figures look blurry and my brain doesn't seem to be working properly. Eventually the bell rings and, waiting for the others to leave, I take my time to close my book and note-book, gather my things, and exit the room.

I'm trying to fly under the radar. I'm not even sure why; it just seems like the right thing to do. I suppose I don't want to bump into Harris, not that there's any chance of that since I don't see him anywhere. I actually start to wonder if Harris might be feeling so bad that he stayed home from school. Is it possible?

It's not until I'm on my way to biology, third period, that I realize some people (friends of Harris and Emery) seem to be glancing at me. And unless it's my imagination, they are acting differently. Then, in fourth period, Saundra actually whispers something to Deidre, and the two of them look at me and giggle before they look away. I have no idea what's going on with them, but I do feel worried.

One thing I know for sure, I will not be eating at Harris's table for lunch today. Whether or not he is at school, I do not plan to risk certain humiliation by assuming I'm still welcome there. In fact, as I'm leaving economics class, I decide to just skip lunch altogether. I'll grab a soda from the machine and hide out in the library until fifth period. But as I'm waiting for the stupid machine to drop a can of Coke, Buck comes up and gives me a curious look.

"What's the problem?" I ask him as nonchalantly as possible. He shrugs. "Nothing."

The can finally rolls out, and as I'm reaching for it, Buck comes closer to me, leaning over almost like he's about to tell me a secret.

"Huh?" I look at him in surprise.

"I was just thinking that if I knew what you were really like, I might've gone for you myself, Haley."

"What?"

He chuckles in a nasty way, then turns and saunters off. I'm pretty sure I know what he meant, but I have no idea how he knows about it. For that matter I have no idea what he knows about it. Part of me wants to chase after him and demand that he explain himself. But most of me feels tired . . . and afraid.

I pretend to read a book in the library and actually doze off until I hear the bell ringing. It's time for fifth period. At least none of Harris's friends are in my art class. That's a relief. I arrive early in the art room, gather what I need to continue my watercolor painting, which I will never give to Harris now, take a seat at the usual table, and get to work. It's hard to focus, and after I make a couple of mistakes, which I try to clean up with a tissue and some water, the other kids start trickling in.

"I heard you and Harris broke up," Poppie says flippantly as she dumps her stuff on the table next to me.

I just nod without looking up.

"You're not sad about it, are you?"

I shrug, still keeping my eyes on my painting.

"You knew it would happen, didn't you?"

I look up at her with narrowed eyes. "Maybe you should get your own life to talk about, *okay*?"

She looks surprised. "Excuse me." She takes off her jacket and hangs it on the back of the chair. "Just trying to be social."

"Well, save yourself the breath." I gather up my things so quickly that my jar of water slops onto the table. I swipe it with a sleeve, then head to the back of the room, where I settle at an empty table.

Of course, now I can't focus at all. How is it that everyone knows about Harris and me? And just how much do they know?

"How's your painting coming?" Ms. Flores asks me from behind.

I jump and nearly spill my water jar again. "Uh, okay, I guess."

"I like that reflection of light on the fender." She points to the front of the old blue truck. "Very nice."

"Thanks."

Now she looks concerned. "Is anything bothering you, Haley?"

"Not really."

She slowly nods, like she's doubtful of my answer. "Well, I can see you're a good artist. And if you ever need to talk . . . I mean, I realize it's hard changing schools in the middle of high school. . . . Anyway, I'm a good listener."

My cheeks are flaming red, but I force a weak smile and thank her, hoping she'll hurry up and move on. Does she honestly think I'm going to open up to her—a teacher?

I concentrate on painting blades of grass now. Because it's fairly tedious, this doesn't require quite as much mental energy. Using shades of gold and pale green, I imagine what this grassy meadow might smell like in late August. I imagine myself lying quietly in the grass, watching the blue sky and clouds rolling by. Will I ever have a peaceful experience like that again? Or is my life forever ruined by the horrors of one awful night? How does a person recover from that kind of betrayal?

"Poppie tells me you and Harris broke up," Zach says in an offhanded way, like he thinks I want to talk to him, then plops himself down at my solitary table.

I just give him a very blank stare.

"Oh . . . ?" He blinks like he's offended. "So you're giving me the cold shoulder now?"

I just shrug. Perhaps I will give up speaking altogether, for all the good it does me.

"Let me guess," he continues, unflappable, "Harris dumped you and now you're brokenhearted."

I continue with the silent treatment.

"The thing is, Haley, he's not worth it. Take it from me. I've known Harris since grade school and he's always been too full of himself. In fact, I didn't want to say anything to you before, but Harris is pretty much a selfish jerk."

I suck in a fast breath, controlling myself from speaking something in Harris's defense, which is perfectly ridiculous.

"You know what they say, Haley."

I roll my eyes at him, then look back down to my mixing tray, where what was once a nice golden green has become muddy.

"Easy come, easy go."

I glare at him now.

"Oh, I see I've got your attention. How about another euphemism." His brow creases. "Oh, yeah. There's always more fish in the sea." He smiles, jerking his thumb to his chest. "Like me, for instance."

"Please, leave me alone," I seethe.

"You're handling this all wrong," he continues. "The best way to get even is to live well and act like you've never been hurt.

Don't let them see you crying. Pull yourself up by your boot-straps and all that rot." He laughs in a sarcastic way, like he's questioning his own advice.

I soften slightly. "I know you think you're making me feel better. But you're not."

"That's because you won't let me. You're building up a wall, Haley. If you're not careful, you'll shut yourself in there so tight that you'll never find your way out."

"It's my life."

He nods. "That it is." Now he stands, takes a mock bow, and goes back to the table where Poppie has been watching the whole thing. I see them talking, heads close together, and although I can't hear what they're saying, I can see they're amused. Well, let them be amused. Let the whole school be amused. See if I care.

Finally the bell rings, but as I'm leaving class, Ms. Flores is looking at me with an intensity that makes me wonder if even she knows what happened to me. But that's impossible.

So far I have managed to avoid seeing Harris, but as I come out of PE, I nearly run right into him. I blink, then step back, biting into my lower lip, which is still sore. The pain brings tears to my eyes . . . at least I think it's the pain. But instead of letting him see me like this, I glare at him. I want to tell him I hate him and he is the slime of the earth, but the words won't come out. Instead I just narrow my eyes, shake my head in disgust, and hurry on past him. And as I'm walking, I hear him laugh. At least I think it's him. It's so weird and heartless I almost think I imagined it. What kind of beast is he?

By the end of the day I am emotionally exhausted. Fortunately, my last class is choir and requires little effort on my part. Just open your mouth and pretend to be singing. No one will know.

Unfortunately, several of Emery's friends are also in this class. They're all talking about me now. I don't know what they're saying or how they know what happened, but I have no doubt that everyone knows something.

After class, Libby hurries to catch up with me as I'm leaving. "Wait."

I pause and just look at her. "What?"

"How are you doing?" she says quietly.

I make what feels like about my tenth shrug today.

"I heard what happened."

"What do you mean?" I hold my head high.

"With you and Harris."

"You mean that we broke up?" I actually am curious as to what everyone knows . . . and also how they found out.

"That and a lot more."

I sigh. "Do you mind telling me how much more? Just so I can be on the same page as everyone else."

"You want the details?" She looks surprised.

I shrug again.

Now she seems uncomfortable. She glances around to see if anyone can hear us and lowers her voice. "Everyone is saying that Harris, you know, spent the night at your house and that you kind of, well, freaked out on him."

"Freaked out on him?"

She nods uneasily. "Because he told you that you weren't any good in bed, you know? And then you guys got in a big fight and broke up."

"Oh . . ." I'm trying to absorb this. "And how did this story get out? I mean, how did everyone find out so quickly about this so-called big fight and all?"

She holds up her iPhone. "Harris texted the whole story to Cal and he forwarded it to Saundra and, well, you know how that goes."

I want to set Libby straight and somehow clear my name, except no words come to me, and I'm on the verge of tears again.

"I just thought you deserved to know the truth," she tells me.

"Right," I mutter. "The *truth*." I just shake my head and walk away.

She calls out to me but I keep on going. I head straight for the nearest exit and hurry out, and then I jog all the way home. When I get to the condo, I'm breathless and crying so hard that my side and my stomach ache.

I wish I were dead.

CHAPTER 13

I've heard of date rape before, but it always sounded like something weird and ugly and out of control—something that would never happen to a girl like me. Even now I question whether that's what really happened or not. To be fair, I think I may have sort of led Harris on by dressing provocatively, inviting him into the condo, consuming alcohol with him, kissing him, and letting him take me into the bedroom . . . so how can that be called rape? Or even date rape?

And even if it was date rape, what am I supposed to do about it now? Harris has already spun his story all over the school—everyone believes him. Even if I could open my mouth, which I seriously doubt, it would be his word against mine. My stomach growls, reminding me that I missed lunch and only had juice for breakfast. I fix a bowl of cold cereal, and as I eat it, I attempt to think clearly. I usually consider myself to be fairly smart and on top of things, but I can't seem to figure this thing out. Mostly I just want to escape it. I want to run and hide.

I put the bowl in the dishwasher, then go to my room, climb into bed, pull the covers over my head, and close my eyes. If I can't just die, I want to will myself to sleep for about a hundred years. Or at least until I'm an adult and can leave on my own and begin a new life without this kind of torment.

I wake up around seven and am not surprised that Dad's not home yet. He usually works late. At first this annoyed me, but now I think it's a blessing in disguise. One problem with Mom was that she had too much time on her hands. She was always hovering over me, asking questions, making accusations, and hatching plans to lock me safely away. Of course, in light of what I've done with my newfound freedom, a part of me wonders if Mom might've been right.

I pick up my phone and, in a moment of weakness, dial her number. I'm tempted to hang up on the first ring except she has caller ID and she might already know it's me. I remember how the last time I called her, shortly after Dad got me this phone, she laid into me about how a cell phone would only get me into trouble.

"Hello?" Her voice comes through loud and clear.

"Hi, Mom." I hope she can't hear the tremor in my voice.

"What's wrong, Haley?"

"Nothing's wrong, Mom. I just wanted to call and say hey."

"Hey? You mean hello?"

"Yeah, hello."

"Is something wrong?"

"No, Mom. Sorry, maybe I shouldn't have called."

"What's your father doing?"

"Right now?"

"Yes, right now."

"He's working?"

"At home?"

"No, at work."

"So he left you home alone?"

"Mom, I'm sixteen."

"Precisely. You're sixteen and home alone at night. Doesn't your father realize what kind of trouble a teen girl can get into if she's left home alone?"

"Oh, Mom." I let out an exasperated sigh but at the same time realize she's right.

"Why is he working at night? Is his job in jeopardy?"

"No, not at all." I try to think. "He just had something he needed to take care of. He should be home anytime now."

"Well, let's hope so. I told you over and over, Haley, your father does not know how to parent. He does not want to parent. He abandoned you and Sean, and why you chose to go live with him defies all reason."

"How is Sean?" I ask, hoping this will change the subject.

"The same. He won't go to church with me. I don't know what's wrong with you kids. The Bible says that if you raise a child in the way he should go, he won't depart from it, but you two children certainly departed. However, I lay the blame for that at your father's feet. You're both following in his wicked footsteps."

"Well, I just wanted to say . . . hello. . . . I should probably go. I have homework to do."

"How are your grades?"

"I haven't been here long enough to know, Mom."

"Well, you better stay on top of your studies. Not that your father will be any help in that department. You chose to be on your own when you left. As my mother used to say, you made your bed and now you'll have to lie in it."

"Yes, I know." I glance over at my unmade bed — the same bed where Harris raped me just two nights ago. "I'll talk to you later, Mom. Please tell Sean hello for me."

We hang up and I begin to cry all over again. Why on earth did I think talking to Mom could possibly make anything better? It only made everything worse. Whether she's right or wrong . . . I'm not even sure. What I do know is her words are like knives slicing into fresh wounds. I so don't need that.

I attempt to do some homework, which is a challenge since I left some of the books I need in my locker. But now I'm thinking about that anonymous warning letter I got last week. I wish I had saved it and I'm trying to remember exactly what it said . . . and how it said it. At the time I thought it was from Emery or one of her friends, trying to scare me away from Harris. Now I wonder if it was written in sincerity. It seemed like it was written by a girl, so maybe someone else has been through something like this with Harris.

I do recall Libby mentioning how Harris was unfaithful to Emery last summer. Was it possible he did something like this then, too? Too many questions and not enough answers.

Dad comes into the house around ten. I go out to say a perfunctory hello — mostly so I can retire back to my room on the pretense of going to bed.

"Sorry to be so late," he tells me. "Tyson at work talked me into a racquetball game and I didn't think it'd last so long." He lets out a tired sigh. "I'm beat."

"Me, too. I just came out to say good night."

He smiles. "You're a good kid, Haley."

I just nod, then turn and go back to my room. A "good kid" whose life is seriously messed up. I briefly wonder what my dad would do if I told him what happened on Saturday night. But I think I can guess . . . it would make him extremely uncomfortable and ruin everything.

One thing I decide as I get ready for bed is that I'd like to find out who wrote that warning letter. I'm just not sure how to go about it. I really don't enjoy talking to anyone at school — at least not about Harris. Still, I feel like if I could get to the bottom of that letter . . . well, maybe it would help.

· · · · · · · · · ·

My second day at school (following the incident) isn't much better than the first. I would think people would find something or someone else to talk about, but they seem to be primarily interested in me. I feel like a shadow as I walk down the halls, keeping my eyes down, not speaking to anyone. Even when I venture into the cafeteria at lunchtime, I keep to myself, getting a cheeseburger and finding an isolated table in a corner.

Unfortunately it's not isolated enough to keep me from seeing Harris's table. And I'd have to be blind not to see that it looks like he and Emery are getting back together again. I'm sure that makes Emery very happy. Now she'll have an escort for homecoming. I hurry to wolf down my burger, quickly escaping outside, where I almost feel like I can breathe again. Will this ever get any easier?

I don't know what to do or where to go. Mostly I'd like to go home, climb into bed, and just sleep. Sleep seems my only escape. But since I have art next, I head over to the art room. Hopefully, no one will be there and I can hide for a while. But I'm barely in the room when Ms. Flores calls out hello from her office.

"Oh, hi," I call back. "Do you mind that I came early?"

She smiles. "Not at all."

I just nod, making my way to my art locker, where I retrieve my current project and carry it to the far back table. Then I go to the front of the class to gather my supplies, and Ms. Flores comes out of her office.

"I can't help but notice that you seem sad, Haley." She looks closely at me. "I mean, compared to when you first came here. You seemed happier then, more confident. Is something troubling you?"

I don't know how to respond. I'm not used to a teacher being this tuned in. Most of them seem to want to get the job done and get out. But Ms. Flores seems like she really cares. "I, uh, I guess I've had some boy troubles."

"Oh." She nods. "Well, that can be a bummer. I'm sorry."

Tears come to my eyes now and I'm not sure why. Maybe it's just her sympathy that's getting to me. "Yeah —" My voice breaks. "I'm kind of having a hard time with it."

"Like I said, I'm a good listener."

"Thanks." I use my hands to wipe the tears that are streaking down. "It's just that, uh, I don't think I can talk about it right now." I glance at the clock, seeing that it's only ten minutes until class. "I mean without falling apart."

"Well, whenever you're ready, Haley, I'm here."

"Thanks."

I feel like a drowning person who's just been thrown a life preserver — and I know I should grab it. But I just can't. Something in me just can't say the words out loud. It would sound so ugly and nasty and disgusting. How will I ever be able to speak those horrid words to anyone? And what will happen when I do?

I go back to my table and begin to work, hoping I can lose myself in the painting. A break would be nice. But as the other kids trickle in, Poppie and Zach relocate themselves to my table.

"Why are you sitting back here?" I demand.

"Why are you?" Poppie shoots back.

"Maybe I just want to be alone."

"That's not very social." Zach pulls out a chair and makes himself comfortable.

I just shake my head. "Whatever."

"Hey, that's looking good," Poppie tells me.

"Thanks," I mutter.

Zach points to where I'm working on the truck's license plate. "Really nice detail there, Haley. You look like you've done this before."

I just shrug. "Thanks."

"See, we're not so bad." Zach sets up his own tools.

"Have you decided what you're going to demonstrate yet?" Poppie asks me.

"Huh?" I look up, confused. "Demonstrate?"

"At the fall art fair. Remember you volunteered? That means you get to demonstrate one of the medias. I'm going to do acrylics and Zach is doing block printing."

"You could do watercolors," Zach tells me.

"Or pottery," Poppie says. "No one's signed up for that yet."

"But maybe she's not into pottery," Zach says, almost like I'm not there.

"As a matter of fact, I am into pottery," I inform them.

"Are you any good?" Zach asks.

"I'm okay."

So now Zach goes up and tells Ms. Flores that I'm a potter, and the next thing I know I'm signed up to demonstrate pottery making on the wheel. "The art fair is two weeks away," Ms. Flores tells the class. "And I'd like to have some of your work ready to be displayed a few days before the show, so if you have pieces that need matting or framing or whatever, please make sure you plan ahead for how you'll handle that."

Then she comes over to where I'm sitting and places a hand on my shoulder. "Haley, do you have any finished pottery pieces you can bring for the show?"

I look up from my painting. "I, uh, I didn't bring anything when I moved down here to live with my dad. I suppose I could ask my mom to send some to me, but she might not—"

"I have a better idea. Why don't you come in here after school and make a few pieces? I assume you're comfortable throwing pots, right?"

I nod, without admitting I was considered one of the best potters in my old school.

"Great." She smiles. "The sooner you get on it, the better the chances your pieces will be glazed and fired in time for the show. Want to come in this afternoon to get started?"

I shrug. "I guess."

"Perfect." She gives my shoulder a squeeze, then goes across the room to help another student.

I'm still trying to figure out how I got roped into this, but, strangely enough, I don't really mind. Maybe it will be a distraction to my troubles. I continue painting, vaguely listening as Poppie and Zach chat and banter about this and that, nothing that interests me too much. But to my surprise I'm disappointed when the bell rings. I think this is the first time I've come close to enjoying myself since that horrible night with Harris. I suppose it should give me hope.

But I'm on my way to my next class when I see something that turns my stomach upside down. I'm just coming around the corner of the senior locker bay when I spy the back of Harris. In his arms is Emery and they are kissing.

Hoping no one sees me, I spin around and go the opposite direction. I duck into the restroom, head straight for the stall, and cannot decide whether I'm going to cry or hurl. As it turns out, I do both. I stay in there several minutes until I hear the bell ring, then dash out and hurry to PE, knowing that if I get ready and in line before roll call, I won't be marked tardy.

At the end of the day, I feel exhausted again. All I want to do is go home and go to bed and sleep and sleep. But I remember my promise to Ms. Flores and for some reason that matters to me. So, feeling like zombie girl, I trudge back to the art department.

"Oh, I'm so glad you're here," Ms. Flores tells me as I enter the art room. "I was hoping you wouldn't forget. I wanted to show you around the pottery room before I go to a staff meeting." Then she gives me a fast tour and I assure her that it's not much different than my old school, and she heads off to her meeting.

I've just sliced off a slab of clay and am vigorously wedging it, slamming it down again and again, far more than necessary since I know any air bubbles are long gone by now, but it feels good to whack it down on the block.

"Sounds like someone's getting her aggressions out in here."

I look up to see Zach watching me from the doorway. Without saying anything I pick up the lump of clay and begin slapping it into a large ball.

"Not that I blame you. I'd be mad too."

"Mad about what?" I push a strand of hair from my eyes as I study him.

With his woodblock and a carving tool in hand, he comes over to a workbench, pulls out a stool, and sits down. "Mad about the way Harris treated you."

I just shrug and continue smoothing out the ball of clay.

"I'm curious about how much you know about Harris . . ."

This sounds like a leading question and, although I hate giving him the satisfaction of my curiosity, I can't help myself. "What do you mean?" I slam the ball of clay onto the wheel — *bull's-eye.*

"Well, you obviously know about Harris and Emery."

I roll my eyes at him as I turn on the wheel, then dip my hands into water and hold them over the clay.

"I mean their history, Haley. Do you know anything about the history between those two?"

I shrug, keeping my eyes on the clay as I pull it taller.

"They've been a couple on and off for several years. They go together happily for a fairly long period of time — then bam, they break up. And shortly after they break up, Harris takes out another girl."

I glance up at him as I dip my hands in water again.

"Harris stays with the new girl a couple of days or maybe even a couple of weeks, but eventually, he and Emery get back together again."

I frown as I push my thumbs into the cylinder of clay, gently pulling the side out, widening it into a bowl.

"It's a pattern. And from what I hear, it's a twisted, sick pattern."

I remove my hands from the clay and study him. "What do you hear?"

"Just that Harris gets what he wants from the other girl and when he's done with her, he goes back to Emery."

I look back down at the clay and wish I'd never asked. I put my hands back onto the clay now, but they're trembling and I go off center and, just like that, what was becoming a nice bowl turns into a deformed, ugly mess.

Kind of like my life.

To my relief, Zach says nothing as I grab the wire and cut the mess off of the wheel, then wad it into a ball, which I feel like hurling at Zach.

"I'm not telling you this to hurt you, Haley. Most of the girls in school know not to get involved with Harris during these mini-breakups; it never turns out well for them."

"Oh . . ." I try not to allow any emotion into my voice as I scrape the wheel clean of clay. "So I must look like the Mitchell High village idiot now."

I give the wheel a quick scrub with a damp sponge, toss the tools back in the toolbox, then walk out. Maybe Zach means well, but his words feel like salt in my wound. If I wanted more pain, I'd go bang my head against the wall.

On my way home, I think about what Zach was telling me. I also think about the warning letter I received and about Emery's words, telling me she would eventually get Harris back. Obviously, she knew what she was talking about. A few questions rumble through my mind. If Harris really likes Emery, like he seems to, why does he break up with her like that? And why was he so attracted to me? And was nothing he said to me true?

Mostly I wonder, does he feel any guilt or responsibility over what happened to me? And if not, why not?

· · · · · · · · · ·

The following day, I do better in the art room after school. I manage to throw a decent pot and two fairly nice bowls, and Ms. Flores seems pleased.

"These are very good, Haley. Thanks for hanging in there and getting it done."

"Yeah . . . I just couldn't get it together yesterday."

"Zach told me why you left."

I blink, then turn away.

"Like I said, I'm a good listener. If you feel the need to talk, I'm always around after school."

I just nod as I wash my hands, carefully scrubbing them clean.

"I hate to be pushy, but sometimes it helps to get things out into the open. Sometimes in the light of day, problems don't seem so bad."

"Thanks." I turn and force a smile. "I'll keep that in mind." Then I grab my sweatshirt and hurry out of there.

For some reason, I think this woman could break me. Her sincere blue eyes and easy smile are tempting. But at the same time I'm worried that if I actually open my mouth to talk about what happened, it will come spewing out of me in the worst sort of way—and it will be repugnant and sickening and poison to anyone who's forced to hear it.

Before I leave the building, I rush into the women's restroom for a quick stop, and as I'm coming out of the stall, I'm shocked to see Emery entering the bathroom. She looks almost as shocked to see me as I am to see her. But she quickly recovers.

"Hello, Haley," she says politely.

"Hey," I say quietly.

She's standing in front of the door and, short of plowing her down, there's no easy way out. "How are you doing?"

I shrug, looking down at my shoes, which are splattered with clay mud. "I'm okay."

"You probably won't believe me, but I'm sorry you got caught in the middle of things with Harris and me. I'm sorry you got hurt."

Something in me snaps. "I got *hurt*? Do you have any idea *how* I got hurt?"

She gives me a blank look. "What do you mean?"

"You're right, I did get hurt. Harris hurt me deeply. I don't even know how he can live with himself after what he did to me. For that matter, I don't know how you can live with him."

"I warned you, Haley. I told you he'd eventually come back to me. I wish you would've listened."

Now I'm angry. I step closer, looking directly into her pretty face. "Do you understand who Harris is? Do you know what he did to me?"

She sighs. "I know he used you. I don't like it when he does that. But I do understand."

"You *know* what Harris did to me? And you *understand*?" What sort of horrible person is she? The same kind of monster as Harris?

"You may not have heard this before, Haley, since you're new, but I made a purity pledge." She holds up her left hand and shows me a pretty gold ring with a diamond set in a heart. "You see, *I* am saving myself for marriage."

I feel slightly faint now. What is she saying? What does this mean?

"Harris doesn't always get this—he questions the seriousness of my commitment." She sighs dramatically. "Oh, he'll be patient for a long time, but then he'll think we should have sex, and if he pushes hard enough, it will cause a fight . . . and sometimes we even break up."

I feel like a lightbulb just went on. "So you tell Harris no, and you guys break up so he can go looking elsewhere to get what he wants?"

She nods with a little smile. "Most of the kids know about it by now. It's kind of a joke. An old joke."

"*A joke?*" I shriek. "You think that's a joke?"

She shrugs. "Well, I suppose it's not that funny to you. But, remember, you were warned."

I take in a deep breath. "Oh yes, I was warned; that makes me feel so much better." I hold up my left hand. "And, for your information, I don't have an expensive diamond ring to show off, but I made a pledge too."

She looks surprised.

"And Harris broke that pledge when he raped me."

Her blue eyes open wide and her hand flies to her mouth.

"That's right," I seethe at her. "Harris got me drunk and then he *raped* me. What do you think about *that*? Do you understand *that*?"

"I don't believe you." She narrows her eyes. "You're just trying to get back at him — at us." She steps away from me, almost like she's afraid I might touch and infect her. "You're messed up, Haley. Seriously messed up. Stay away from me."

"You're right about one thing: I *am* messed up. And your boyfriend is the one who messed me up!" I storm past her and out of there. My hands are trembling and my knees are shaking and I feel like I could vomit all over the locker bay. But instead of giving in to this, I jog down the hallway and out the nearest exit and run all the way home.

I get into bed, pull the covers over my head again, and tightly close my eyes, willing all of this to go away. *Leave me alone!* And yet all I see is Emery's smug face as she holds up her left hand to taunt me with her purity pledge ring. I feel like I was the sacrifice for her purity. Like it's *her* fault that my life will never be the same. She remains untouched, a perfect, pristine princess virgin. Meanwhile I am used and soiled and broken . . . *damaged goods.*

· · · · · · · · · ·

Even with a few answers to my mountain of questions, like why Harris used me the way he did, I do not feel one bit better about my situation. I do feel like I need to do something — but what? What can I do to get some resolution? Some peace? What will bring an end to this pain? Or will I wear my cloak of sadness for the rest of my life? I know I should take an active role in making things better, but I don't know what to do.

So instead of doing anything, I continue my zombie-girl routine, going through my days like a walking dead girl, avoiding all conversation, any confrontation, simply going through the paces and wishing I could turn back the clock or sleep for a few years.

On Friday, I feel like an outsider watching a circus. Everyone, it seems, is hyped up over homecoming. Football players are wearing their jerseys, cheerleaders are in their uniforms doing routines in the cafeteria, and there's a pep assembly that I sleep through. Rah-rah-rah — school spirit blah! I'm so not into it.

After school I head to the art room to work on my pottery. I want to trim and clean up my pieces and sign them so they can be fired next week. I'm just finishing up when Ms. Flores comes into the pottery room. "I thought I heard someone in here."

I make a weary smile. "Just getting them ready for their bisque firing."

"Great. I plan to run the kiln on Tuesday or Wednesday."

I set down the last bowl and look at Ms. Flores. "I, uh, I wonder if you'd want to do some listening today?" I ask nervously.

"Of course. Come on into my office."

With my heart pounding wildly, I follow her to her office. I hadn't really planned to do this—it just popped out of my mouth. But maybe it's for the best.

"Have a seat."

I sit down, then nod to her door. "Would you mind closing that?"

"Not at all."

"Thanks." I take in a deep breath, letting it out slowly.

"So, I know this has to do with a boy, Haley. A certain boy who has a bit of a reputation with the girls, correct?"

I nod. "Harris Stephens."

"You were going with him?"

Again I nod. "Just barely. But I thought it was more . . . more than it was."

"And now you're brokenhearted?"

A lump grows in my throat and I will myself not to cry. "Yes," I say in a gruff voice. "But there's actually more to it than that."

She nods. "Why don't you tell me about it?"

So I tell her about how I was teaching him guitar and how it seemed we had something really special. "It's the first time I had that with a guy. I mean, I've kissed a guy before. But this was different. I felt like I loved him . . . and I trusted him."

"First love."

"I guess." Now I bite my lip, wondering if I can really say this out loud. "You see, I'd never really been with a guy, you know. I'd barely even kissed a guy before Harris. And on our second date, which was so perfectly wonderful . . . magical . . . I didn't see how anything about that night could go wrong."

"But something did go wrong?"

I nod.

"What happened, Haley?"

Tears are coming now; it's useless to hold them back. "Harris wanted to come up to the condo after our date, to play guitar, so I said yes. My dad was on a date, so we were alone." I swallow hard.

"I see." She reaches over and puts her hand on my arm. "Don't worry, Haley, there's not much I haven't heard."

"Harris brought some kind of alcohol with him and he wanted to make us drinks. I've never had alcohol before and I really didn't want any, but he insisted . . . and I gave in."

"Did you get drunk?"

"Yes. I think I actually kind of passed out. And then we were in my bedroom . . . and well, he forced me to, you know. . . . I told him no over and over, and I told him not to do that. But he wouldn't listen."

Ms. Flores leans forward in her chair. "He raped you?"

I nod, looking down at my lap.

"Oh, Haley." Her voice is laced with sadness. "I'm so sorry."

Now I'm crying hard and she hands me some tissues. "I . . . I haven't told anyone. I . . . I didn't know what to do or who to talk to."

"So you didn't report it?"

I shake my head no.

"When did it happen?"

"Last Saturday." I can't believe it's been only a week. It feels like a lifetime.

"And you didn't even tell your parents?"

Without going into all the details, I explain about my parents.

"How do you feel about reporting this, Haley?"

"No! I can't do that."

"Why not?"

"It would be so humiliating. And he'd deny it. Then it would be my word against his. I just couldn't go through all that."

"How do you feel about him going around like he's done nothing wrong? I mean, he's put you through so much and he's not being held accountable for any of it."

"I know." I look at her. "I hate that."

"But if you don't speak out—"

"I just can't. It would be too hard."

"But what if Harris does this to someone else? How would you feel about that?"

I sigh. "Horrible."

"And what if you're not the only one he's hurt?"

I tell her what Zach told me about how there's a pattern, how Harris and Emery go together and then break up. I even tell her what Emery told me in the restroom.

"Oh, Haley, that's terrible. Don't you want to try to do something to stop that boy?"

"I wish there was a way to stop him, or punish him, or whatever . . . but without me being involved."

"I don't know how. But I do think you should talk to the counselor. Mrs. Evanston is very easy to talk to. And she'll know how to help you with this."

"I don't think I can do that," I say nervously. "It was hard enough to tell you."

"Mrs. Evanston is very understanding, Haley. I really think you should speak to her."

I blow my nose and just shake my head. "I can't."

"Well, I'm glad you at least told me. And now I can understand why you've seemed so different. This is much more than just a broken heart."

I nod and throw the used tissue in the trash can. "I just want it to go away. The pain, I mean. I just want to be who I was before, you know?"

"Before Harris stole from you." She frowns. "I want you to understand that what he did was a crime. Just the same as if he stole your car, only far worse. Tell me, Haley, if Harris had stolen your car, you'd report him, wouldn't you?"

I stand, ready for this to end and wondering if I was wrong to tell her. "I guess. But this is different."

"Please, think about talking to Mrs. Evanston."

"Okay. . . ." I force a wobbly smile. "And maybe you're right. I do feel a tiny bit better getting it out into the open. . . ." I want to plead with her not to repeat this to anyone, but that might sound like I don't trust her.

She stands with a sad expression. "I hear so many sad stories from my students. Kids can be so hard on each other. I wish I could do more than just listen."

"I appreciate your time." I glance at the clock and am surprised to see it's already past five. "I should probably get home now."

Of course, even as I say this, I know it won't matter when I get home since Dad's going out with Estelle tonight. But I'm guessing Ms. Flores, unlike me, has a life.

Naturally, I don't go to homecoming. I no longer have any interest in football or in being around a bunch of kids from my school. Most of all, I do not want to see Harris . . . or Emery. They both make me sick.

Of course, even as I'm thinking about how much I despise them and how I hope our team loses the game tonight, I still have a hard time believing Harris really did that to me — and that he doesn't still care about me. Sometimes I have an even harder time convincing myself that I no longer care about him. But then I remember that thick black line that divides my feelings about this guy right down the middle. On one side of the line stands pre-Harris and on the other side looms post-Harris. Pre-Harris is a sweet gentleman; he is fun and thoughtful and interesting. Post-Harris is a horrible monster. I suppose it's a bit like the *Strange Case of Dr. Jekyll and Mr. Hyde*, but I can't remember how that book ended.

Did Jekyll kill himself to destroy Hyde, or did Hyde destroy Jekyll?

· · · · · · · · · ·

By Monday I have the assurance (as well as the cramps) to verify that I'm not pregnant. I didn't really think I was, but it's a relief knowing for sure that I am not. Life is complicated enough without having something like *that* to deal with.

The weather this morning is reflective of how I feel—low gray clouds and chilly drizzle. By the time I get to school, my hair is limp and damp and I probably look like something the cat dragged in. Not that I care.

As usual I try to keep a low profile. I've gotten good at staying below the radar. I take the less traveled routes, get to class early, avoid eye contact, and, continuing my zombie-girl routine, make it through another day. Even in art class, I keep to myself. Despite Zach and Poppie's best efforts to engage with me and be "social," I keep a small wall built up around me. I think eventually they will either get the hint or get fed up . . . and find another place to sit.

It does bother me that Harris and Emery seem to live in a protective bubble of friends and popularity (and, yes, they did win their stupid football game last Friday, and, yes, Emery was crowned homecoming queen and Harris escorted her). But it irks me to no end knowing they are totally oblivious to the pain I'm in—the pain they continue to heap upon me simply by breathing the same air.

In fact, today I had to leave the cafeteria before I threw up when I saw those two spoiled brats dancing together (actually it looked like dirty dancing to me). They were obviously showing off in front of their friends, who were clapping and laughing.

Truly, it was nauseating and I went directly to the restroom in the fear that I was about to lose what little lunch I'd been able to consume. But after a bit, I realized I was okay — or as okay as one can be under the circumstances. Will I ever really be okay?

And in moments like that little scene in the cafeteria, I really want to tell the world about the real Harris — I want everyone (even his parents) to know what kind of person he actually is. I want everyone to know that Emery's boyfriend is a rapist — and that even though she's aware of this, she still goes out with him, pretending he's her wonderful Prince Charming. They should've crowned her the Homecoming Queen of Denial.

But what can I do about anything? It's not like I want to go public and suffer even further humiliation. Besides, who would believe me? A newcomer's word against the golden-boy football hero? Still, if there was a way to anonymously blow this whistle, I feel fairly certain that I would.

By Thursday I feel a tiny bit stronger. I'm not even sure why. Unless it's like the old saying that "time heals all wounds." But a little bit of the sting is gone, and I feel like I can walk with just a tiny bit more confidence.

Part of this is the result of Ms. Flores' praise and appreciation for what I'm contributing to the fall art fair, which is next week. My pottery went through its final firing and the glazes I chose turned out very nicely. Even I felt proud. Also, my watercolor of the old truck in the field is finished and Zach helped me cut some mats that really show it off nicely. All things considered, it is an okay sort of day.

But then Friday comes, and for some reason I feel a sense of foreboding as I go to my first class. I have no idea where this feeling is coming from, but by second period I know my instincts are accurate when I am asked to report to the office. I don't know why I feel so uncomfortable (almost guilty) as I walk down there — I have done nothing wrong. But when the receptionist sends me to the office of Mrs. Evanston and two other adults are already waiting there, I have cause to be distressed.

"Hello, Haley," Mrs. Evanston says. She has kind dark eyes and what seems a sympathetic smile. "Please take a seat."

I barely nod, then sit in the chair across from her desk, my knees shaking. I have never been in any kind of real trouble, but for some reason this feels like something very serious.

"You're probably wondering why we've called you down here."

Again I nod, swallowing against the hard lump in my throat.

"Let me introduce you to Detective Harbick." She points to the middle-aged man in a gray blazer. "And Detective Dorman." She points to a younger woman in a navy suit. Both of them smile stiffly at me.

Suddenly my stomach feels like I swallowed a brick for breakfast. "Wh-what is going on?" I ask in a mousy voice.

"According to California law, teachers are required to report it if they believe a crime has been committed." Mrs. Evanston clears her throat. "Ms. Flores spoke to me on Wednesday. She explained to me about what happened to you."

"She told?" I peer helplessly at Mrs. Evanston. *"Why?"*

"As I said, according to California law, teachers are obligated to report it if a crime against a minor has been committed. If it makes you feel any better, she didn't want to tell. She knew you were trying to deal with it on your own, Haley. But it was her responsibility to report it. Her job could've been at risk if she hadn't."

"And what you may not understand," the woman cop steps in, "is that by *not* reporting a crime, you are essentially allowing a perpetrator not only to go free but also to possibly commit the same crime again on another victim."

"Detective Dorman's right," the man confirms. "And crimes

like rape, particularly date rape, are sometimes committed by repeat offenders."

I feel slightly dizzy now. Leaning over, I put my head in my hands and tears slip down my cheeks. "I can't do this," I mutter into my lap. "I cannot do this. Please do not make me do this."

I feel a hand on my shoulder and glance over to see that it's bronze colored, which tells me it's Mrs. Evanston. "I know this is going to be hard, Haley, but hasn't it already been pretty hard on you? I've spoken to all your teachers, and a number of them confirm that you've been acting differently these past couple of weeks. You're obviously in pain."

I look up at her with tears running down my face. "But it will be so humiliating," I whisper. "How can I talk about *that* to — to anyone?"

"We'll try to do this in whatever way makes you most comfortable, Haley," Detective Dorman tells me. And Mrs. Evanston hands me some tissues.

"If you like, I can step out," the man says quietly.

I just nod, looking back down at my lap and feeling like a bug under a magnifying glass as I blow my nose.

"They wanted to take you to the station to get your statement," Mrs. Evanston explains to me, "but I encouraged them to do it here. However, if you'd prefer to go down —"

"No, I don't want to go to a police station."

Mrs. Evanston tips up the blinds on her windows so no one can see in. I take a deep breath, and for the first time since my ordeal began, I feel like whispering a prayer to God. However, I do not. Partly because I have a feeling he's not listening and partly because Detective Dorman is asking me if I mind if she records my statement.

"I guess not."

She turns on a small device, sets it on the desk, then asks me to state my full name, address, and parents' names. I give her that information as well as answering some other perfunctory questions. Mrs. Evanston gives me a bottle of water.

"Now tell me about you and Harris. Were you and he a couple? Or was this just a one-time date?"

I explain about how we were friends, how he wanted guitar lessons, and then about how he and Emery broke up. "He seemed to really like me. We were together at school and he gave me rides, and I thought we were a couple. But we only had two actual dates. I mean, where we went out, you know, and had dinner and stuff. But we'd done some other things together too."

"During this time did you ever have consensual sex with Harris?"

"No, *never*!"

"But you were romantic together?"

"Yes."

"Can you describe your relationship? Did you kiss or touch each other?"

My face gets hot. "We kissed. I guess you could say we kissed a lot."

"Anything else?"

"Harris would kind of try some things . . . you know . . ." I glance at Mrs. Evanston and she just nods as if encouraging me to continue. "And I would kind of make him stop." Then I tell them about the time we were in his car at the lookout point. "I was relieved that the cop came. It felt like too much."

"Have you had any other boyfriends?"

"No. I had an *almost* boyfriend at my other school, but all we did was kiss, and then my mom found out and that was the end of it."

"I spoke to the counselor at your other school," Mrs. Evanston says. "She said that you were considered a very serious and academic student there and that you never got into any sort of trouble." She frowns. "But she also mentioned that your mother worried quite a bit about you getting into trouble."

"My mother is a little . . . well, she's kind of fearful about a lot of things."

"The counselor said something to that effect."

"If my mother had her way, I'd be dressing like a nun and going to private church school," I confess. "That's why I petitioned the court to live with my dad and it's why the judge ruled in my favor."

"So back to Harris," the detective says. "When did he rape you?"

"On our last date." I tell her when that was.

"Can you describe that night?"

"It started out as a really special date. Nice dinner, candles, and everything. We took a walk in the park. It was magical." Even as I say this, I find it hard to believe that something so wonderful turned out to be so horrific.

"So when and where did the rape happen?"

"In my bedroom."

"Was anyone else at home?"

I explain that Dad was out.

"Did you *invite* Harris into your house?"

"He asked if he could come in. He had his guitar, and I'd been giving him lessons. We were just going to play some music."

"Did you play music?" The detective is studying me now. I can only imagine what she's thinking.

"We played for a while, then he stopped and I played a little longer."

"Then what happened?"

I explain about the alcohol. "He told me it was mostly Coke, but I think whatever was in it hit me kind of hard."

"Do you usually drink alcohol?"

"No, never. It was the first time."

"So, Harris brought the alcohol with him?"

"It was in his guitar case."

"But you willingly drank some. Do you recall how much you drank?"

"Not really. I remember he refilled my glass, or maybe he gave me his glass. It's all pretty fuzzy now."

"Were you intoxicated?"

"I think so. I think I must've blacked out . . . because I came to in my bedroom and I couldn't even remember how we got there."

"You didn't willingly go to your bedroom then?"

"No way. What if my dad came home?"

She nods, looking down at the notepad in her lap. "Now I'll need you to go into more detail, Haley. I know it's not comfortable getting this personal, but this is information we need."

She asks me more specific questions, and although my face gets hotter and hotter, I try to answer. But some of the things she says don't even make sense. I don't even know what she's talking about. Finally she asks if Harris used protection.

"I honestly don't know. After he wouldn't quit, I just closed my eyes." I reach up and touch my lip, which has healed. "And I bit into my lip so hard it looked like someone had hit me."

"Did he hit you?"

"No." I shake my head.

"Did you take a photo of your lip or did anyone see you?"

"No to the photo. But my dad saw it and I told him I'd hit it while swimming laps in the pool."

"So when Harris was done, what did you do?"

I describe how he fell asleep and I just waited to be sure. "Then I grabbed my underwear and ran to the bathroom and took a really long shower." I tell her how I barricaded myself in there and when I finally came out, he was gone.

"You mentioned that you grabbed your underwear, Haley. What did you do with it?"

A jolt hits me. "I, uh, I wanted to destroy it. And the dress I'd been wearing, because it was torn too. They were both too damaged to wear again."

"Did you destroy them?"

"No. I totally forgot. I wadded them into a ball and hid them beneath the sink in my bathroom. As far as I know, they're still there."

Detective Dorman looks pleased. "That's good news. Those items are evidence." She asks me about what happened the following day. "Did you tell anyone what happened to you?"

I shake my head. "No one."

"So your parents don't know."

"The only one I told was Ms. Flores." Now I remember something. "And Emery Morrison."

"Is that your best friend?"

I frown. "No. That's Harris's girlfriend."

"Girlfriend?"

So I explain that.

"Interesting." Now she looks confused. "But you told this girl that Harris raped you?"

I tell her the story of meeting Emery in the restroom. I even tell her about the purity pledge ring. And then I remember the warning letter I received and tell her about that.

"Do you still have the letter?"

"No . . . at the time I thought someone, like one of Emery's friends, was just trying to scare me away from Harris. So I burned it." Now I remember how Emery had warned me herself, saying that Harris would eventually go back to her, so I tell the detective about that, too. "And I even had a couple of other warnings." I mention Poppie and Zach's concern. "Zach even suggested that this is a pattern with Harris. And I suppose he could be right."

Detective Dorman turns to Mrs. Evanston. "Do you suppose there could be other girls at this school who've been caught up in this? I mean, if it really is a pattern."

"It's possible, but I don't know how we'd ever find out."

Now I remember Libby mentioning something about a time when Harris and Emery broke up and he had another girlfriend. So I tell them this and the detective makes note of it. She asks a few more questions and finally announces she's done.

"What will happen now?" I ask nervously.

"We'll bring Harris in for questioning."

I take in a slow breath. "So he'll know I talked to you."

She nods.

"There's no way to do this anonymously?"

"I'm sorry. I wish there were. But we will try to protect you as much as we can, Haley."

Now I'm crying again. "I don't know if I can do this."

"Do what?" Mrs. Evanston asks.

"Go to this school with everyone knowing about it — knowing I'm the one who got their star football player in trouble."

"He's a star football player?" Detective Dorman asks.

"He's the quarterback," Mrs. Evanston explains. "And the team's having a good year."

The detective gives me a sympathetic look. "It won't be easy. I suppose you could look into transferring to another school."

This reminds me about Dad. "And will you tell my dad?"

"He'll have to know, Haley. We can tell him or you can tell him. But he has to know."

I shake my head and look down at my hands in my lap. This is so hard.

"One more thing."

I look up. "What?"

"Let's run by your house and pick up that evidence. Okay?"

I shrug. "I guess."

Then I'm dismissed to wait with the other detective while the two women go over a few more things.

"Are you okay?" Detective Harbick asks in a gentle tone.

"I guess." I look at the clock to see that it's almost time for lunch. "Uh, Detective Dorman said you guys are going to take me home to get some, uh, evidence."

"Okay."

I point to the clock. "Is there any chance we could get out of here before the other kids are on their way to lunch? I really don't want to be seen going out with . . . well, you know."

"Sure." He ducks his head into the office and explains that he and I will wait in the car. Then we quickly hurry out and I hope that if anyone does see me, they'll assume he's my dad.

Hopefully my dad will be as understanding as this cop.

I'm not sure if I'm relieved or not when I discover that my wad of clothes is still under the sink, but I hand it over to Detective Dorman and she slips it into a bag.

"I have a question," I say timidly as I walk her to the door.

"Yes?"

"What if I don't want to press charges against Harris?"

She puts a hand on my shoulder. "I know this is hard to hear, but it's out of your hands. Because you're a minor, it's up to the district attorney to prosecute, not you. Even if you refused to cooperate with us, we would still pursue this. But, trust me, it will be easier if you continue to cooperate . . . like you did today."

I bite my lip and wish this would all just go away.

"I know this is difficult. I do understand. But what you need to understand is that by doing this, you might be sparing another girl. Maybe more than one girl, because if a guy gets away with this once, he might think he can do it again . . . and again. Wouldn't you feel terrible if you said nothing and years later learned that Harris Stephens was a serial rapist? Or perhaps worse?"

I consider this. "Yes. You're right, I would."

"So hang in there." She makes a half smile. "And tell your dad what happened."

"I . . . I'll try."

"Because he will find out. It's just a matter of how and when."

. . . .

I decide to tell Dad first thing when I see him, but as usual, he goes out with Estelle on Friday night and comes home late. Then when I get up on Saturday morning, it feels like he's going to sleep in forever. Should I even bother? Really, what does he care?

When he finally gets up, it seems like he's in a bad mood. Not grumpy bad, just very quiet. It almost feels like he's avoiding me, or maybe he just doesn't want to talk to anyone, or maybe he has a hangover, although I hope that's not the reason. But what if it *is* me? What if the police called him and told him the whole thing? Suddenly I'm worried. Does Dad already know?

"Want some coffee?" I recently started both making and drinking coffee. My mother would hate this, but for some reason I find caffeine to be calming.

"Thanks," he mutters as he shuffles into the kitchen.

I fill a mug and hand it to him. Even though I've already had my coffee, I pour another cup and sit at the breakfast bar, watching as he forages the fridge for food.

"Is everything okay?" I ask tentatively as he puts slices of bread in the toaster.

He shrugs.

Now I feel really nervous. He must know. Why else is he acting like this? I watch as he butters his toast, then liberally smears it with peanut butter and jelly (his version of a quick, healthy breakfast).

"I guess I should just tell you." He sits across from me.

"Tell me?" My stomach sinks.

He nods.

I wait, holding my breath.

"Estelle and I broke up."

"Oh?" I feel a shiver of relief.

He takes a large bite, noisily chewing.

"I . . . I'm sorry, Dad. Are you feeling pretty bad about it?"

"A little. But I'm the one who broke it off."

"*You* broke it off?"

He lets out a sad sigh. "I have to admit Estelle was a nice distraction for a while, when I was lonely and needed something. And she was definitely fun. But I really wasn't in love with her. It seemed like the relationship was going nowhere. And she always expected more than I could give." He sighs. "It was time to call it quits."

"How did she take it?"

"Oh, you know . . . she was unhappy. Maybe even mad. But it really seemed the best—for both of us. And I felt bad for neglecting you too, Haley. Oh, I know we had that *let's be grown-ups* thing going on, but I just don't feel good about it. I mean, you're only sixteen. And you might not think you need any parenting, but I realized I might need to be a dad. After all, you're going to be heading off to college in less than two years and I've already missed so much." He makes a goofy grin. "You think you still have room in your life for your daddy?"

My chin is quivering and I'm about to burst into tears, but I'm trying very hard not to. However, the lump in my throat feels like the size of a grapefruit and I know I can't hold back.

"Sorry, honey." Dad looks alarmed. "Did I say something wrong?"

"No . . . no," I blurt. "It's just . . . just . . . oh, I don't know. . . ." I jump from the stool and run to my room, where I burst into full-blown sobs. I'm not even sure why I'm crying exactly. On one hand I'm relieved that Dad and Estelle broke up, but on the other hand I realize that what I have to tell him will probably hurt him too. At the very least he'll be disappointed in me for making such poor choices.

After a couple of minutes, I hear a *tap-tap* on my door. "Come in," I say in a hoarse voice as I sit up in bed.

Dad opens the door and hesitantly enters my room. "What's going on?" he asks with concerned eyes.

Naturally this brings on more tears. Why is it that sympathy breaks me down like this? "It's a long story."

He pulls a chair closer to my bed and sits down. "I'm not going anywhere."

I put some pillows behind me and lean into the headboard of my bed, closing my eyes. "This isn't going to be easy, Dad."

"Take your time."

"It's very humiliating," I admit with my eyes still closed. "And I know you'll be disappointed in me."

Now there's a pause and I wonder if I'm scaring him, but I keep my eyes closed, hoping that maybe he'll just leave.

"You need to remember something, Haley."

I open my eyes and look at him. He's leaning forward with his hands resting on his knees. "I am not your mother. She and I think completely differently about things. I'll admit that I have my faults—plenty of them—but one thing I won't do is judge you. Do you understand what I'm saying?"

I nod, trying not to cry again.

"Honestly, Haley, there is nothing you can tell me that will make me love you any less. You could tell me you cheated on your math test or slept with your boyfriend or robbed a liquor store or got a tattoo or decided you prefer girls to boys or have become addicted to drugs or whatever. I'll still be your dad and I'll still love you. Okay?" He peers at me. "Do you get that?"

I nod.

"In fact, if we're making confessions, I should tell you that I'm very sorry for what a lousy dad I've been to you since you got here. But that's going to change now."

Again there's a long silence, but hearing him say all that — how I could do anything and he'd still love me — makes me feel stronger. Like I can do this. "Well, I haven't robbed any liquor stores. But what happened does involve the police." I wait, watching as he simply nods. Then I slowly begin and, amazingly, just tell him the whole story.

As I talk, he is kind of twisting his fingers around, as if he's nervous or upset but trying to act cool. Finally, when I am done, he stands up and begins pacing. Pounding his fist into his palm, he looks very angry.

"I'm sorry, Dad." I feel tears coming. "I never meant for that to happen and I know now that I never should've let Harris in here without you —"

"No!" Dad turns and looks at me, and I'm shocked to see tears in his eyes. I've only seen this man cry once before and that was when he left Mom. "That's not why I'm mad, Haley. I am enraged at Harris. I want to kill him!" He pounds his fist again. "I really want to make that boy suffer!"

I blink in surprise.

"Oh, don't worry, I'm not going to charge over to his house and take the law into my own hands, but I am going to back you in this legal case. That boy deserves to be prosecuted — fully."

Then I explain how there's not much evidence.

"Why didn't you tell me when this happened?"

"I was so scared . . . and ashamed . . . and you weren't home. I didn't know what to do. I would've called Mom, but you know how that would've gone. In fact, I did call her a few days later . . . and she was still the same. I couldn't tell her."

Dad comes over and takes my hands in his hands, looking into my eyes. "I'm sorry I was so checked out, Haley. I feel like this is partially my fault."

"It's okay, Dad. I should've known better."

"This is *not* your fault, Haley. Do you get that? It's not your fault. That boy was way out of line. What he did was wrong. You can't blame yourself."

"Maybe not. But I know I'll never do that again. I'll never get into a situation like that again."

"Oh, honey, I sure hope not." He sniffs. "You're such a beautiful girl—inside and out. You didn't deserve to be treated like that. No one does."

Once again, his sympathy brings on my tears. I remind him about my purity pledge; I made it before the divorce so he knows about it. "But now the pledge is ruined. I feel like I'm—*I'm damaged.*"

He squeezes my hands. "You might feel damaged, Haley. But when you get past this, I know you'll be the same sweet girl as before."

I shake my head. "I don't know."

"I'll admit I haven't been going to church since, well, since your mom started going off the deep end and things fell apart. But I still believe in God. Do you?"

I consider this. "I guess so. But I know God must be mad at me. Not for what Harris did, but because I was so stupid to—"

"I disagree," he says firmly. "I don't believe God is like that. The God I believe in is loving and kind and forgiving."

I take in a long, deep breath. "I'd like to believe that too, Dad."

"Well, I have an idea. I'm not saying it's going to solve all our problems. But a guy at work keeps inviting me to his church. It's right here in Mitchell and it's a nondenominational church where it sounds like everyone is welcome. According to Ryan, it's very positive and the music is uplifting. Maybe you and I should give it a try tomorrow. You want to?"

I shrug. "Okay."

Now Dad hugs me, long and hard. "Oh, Haley, I would do anything to take all that away from you. I'm really sorry I wasn't here."

After he lets me go, I admit how I'd wanted him to walk in and catch Harris and rescue me.

He shakes his head. "As much as I wish that had happened, I also know that if it had, I might be the one facing prosecution now." Then he asks about what's being done to Harris.

"I don't really know. It's in the hands of the police. They told me since I'm under eighteen, they have to prosecute him for me. I don't even have a choice in the matter."

"What would you do if you had a choice?"

"I don't know . . . I suppose I might've just buried it." I tell him how Ms. Flores was the one who blew the whistle. "At first I was mad at her. But then I realized she was just doing her job and I forgave her."

"Well, I'm glad she did what she did," Dad assures me. "Harris should not get away with that. The law is the law, no matter how old or young you are."

"I guess so."

We talk a while longer and I feel better than I've felt in days. "Thanks for listening like that," I tell him. "You made it easier."

"Do you need to see a counselor or anything?" he asks with a creased brow. "I mean, I've heard of situations like this where the victim ends up with PTSD."

"Post-traumatic stress disorder?" This makes me think of Sean and all he's been dealing with since he came home. It's hard to believe Sean and I could really be suffering from the same thing.

"Do you think that's possible?"

"I don't really know."

He tilts his head toward my computer. "Maybe we should check it out. Find out what you might be up against. I've always believed that knowledge is power."

"Me, too." So I turn on my computer, Google PTSD, and begin to read. "Look," I tell Dad. "Rape is listed right beneath war." So maybe Sean and I really do share some common ground here. Who would've thought?

"I'm not surprised at that."

I begin to read the list of symptoms aloud. "Bad dreams, fearfulness, feeling numb, difficulty thinking." I nod. "I guess I've had all of those."

"Look at this." He points to a list at the bottom of the page. "Have you had any of these things?"

I silently read this list:

- Anger and irritability
- Guilt, shame, or self-blame
- Substance abuse
- Depression and hopelessness
- Suicidal thoughts and feelings

• Feeling alienated and alone
• Feelings of mistrust and betrayal
• Headaches, stomach problems, chest pain

"Besides substance abuse, I think I've experienced all those things."

"Oh, Haley, I'm so sorry." He puts his arm around my shoulders. "I'd feel better if we got you some kind of counseling. Would you agree to that?"

"I guess."

"I'll do some calling around for you," he tells me. "I have a friend who probably knows a good counselor. In fact, if you don't mind, I think I'll get right on it."

"Thanks, Dad."

He makes a sad smile as he's leaving my room. "I really am sorry for not being here when you needed me."

"It's okay, Dad. You're here now." As he leaves, I wonder if I really need counseling. Already I feel so much better than I did yesterday. Still, it probably can't hurt. Reading that symptom of substance abuse scared me — I can't even imagine how messed up my life would become if I turned to drugs for relief. I don't want to go down that road.

CHAPTER 17

Dad and I go to church together on Sunday, and it's actually a very cool experience. For the first time in a long time, I'm reminded that God really loves me and that he can forgive anything, including my recent silent treatment toward him. This is such a different message than what I've been hearing from my mom these past few years that I'd nearly forgotten the truth.

At the end of the worship service, the pastor invites anyone who wants to make a new commitment or a recommitment to raise their hands, and without even stopping to think about it, my hand shoots up. At first I feel conspicuous, but then I realize I want this. I really want this. A fresh start with God is exactly what I need. A few seconds after I raise my hand, Dad raises his.

After church we go to lunch and we actually talk about the sermon and how it affected us. "I was kind of shocked," I admit to him. "I mean, that I raised my hand to recommit my heart to Jesus. It was like it just happened, like I couldn't even stop myself."

"I get that." He nods eagerly.

"I turned my back on God. I think I used Mom's warped religion as an excuse to put up a wall." I take a sip of iced tea. "I can't believe how stupid that was—to throw away my relationship with God just because Mom painted such a skewed image of him. I thought I was smarter than that."

"But I can understand it, Haley. In some ways, I think I did the same thing."

"That's so sad when someone who's messed up can drag others down the same twisted trail."

"But isn't that exactly what's happened to your mom?" He looks into my eyes with what seems like real empathy . . . for Mom. "Hasn't she been led down the twisted trail too?"

"Yeah . . . you're right." I let out a long sigh. "But if you try to tell Mom that she's going down the wrong trail, she'll just lay into you."

"Believe me, I know." He gets a thoughtful expression as he takes a slow sip of coffee.

"Anyway, I want to start living my life differently," I proclaim. "I want to make choices that honor God." I feel a small rush of enthusiasm. "Like the pastor said, I want a new beginning."

"So do I." Dad grins at me. "Maybe we can help each other, eh?"

I feel a lump in my throat as I nod. "I'd like that." We talk a while longer, discussing the things we want to change in our lives and ways we can encourage each other. It's incredibly cool to have this kind of conversation with my dad, and although I wouldn't go so far as to say I feel really happy (that seems impossible), I do feel hopeful . . . and relatively good.

Sunday evening while reading my Bible, I am faced with my first new spiritual challenge. Reminded of an old foundational truth of Christianity, I realize that just as God forgave me, which was reinforced when I recommitted my life to him today, *I also need to forgive others*. I'd like to convince myself that this doesn't include Harris. Unfortunately, I know better. But right now, the best I can do is ask God to help me with what seems like an impossible task.

Even so, I feel slightly optimistic as I go to school on Monday. I actually took care in getting ready for school today — no more slumming or acting like zombie girl. This is the beginning of my fresh start. However, I'm barely inside the building when I can tell something's wrong. I get this eerie feeling that everyone is talking about me, looking at me, pointing at me, and whispering to each other, and although I try to tell myself this is just paranoia or maybe a symptom of PTSD, somehow I don't think so. This feels real.

Suddenly Emery and several of her friends flock around me in front of my locker. They all look so angry I'm reminded of a lynch mob and wonder if I should make a fast break out of here. But it's too late; I'm surrounded.

"What's going on?" I ask, trying to maintain nonchalance, which is nearly impossible.

"That's what we want to know," Emery says in an accusing tone.

"Why are you running around telling lies to the police?" Saundra demands.

"Did you know you got Harris into some really serious trouble?" Deidre narrows her eyes.

Emery puts her face uncomfortably close to mine. "I know what you're doing, Haley."

"What?" I hold my notebook in front of me like a shield.

"You're trying to ruin Harris's life! You want to take him down. And me with him. And we are not going to stand by and let you get away with it."

"All I did was tell the truth." I close my locker behind me, trying to figure out a way to free myself from this small mob.

"Thanks to your vicious lies, Harris will probably get suspended, and then he won't even be able to play football," Saundra jeers at me. "Thanks to you, we probably won't go to state now."

I stare at her. "You think just because a guy is a football star, he should get a free pass? He should be above the law, allowed to rape girls?"

"You're such a liar," Emery seethes. "You want to ruin our lives just because yours is so pathetic."

"Harris ruined *my* life," I tell her, holding back tears. "What he did was wrong—illegal even. And I wasn't going to tell anyone, but the police forced me to—"

"You just want to hurt Harris," Saundra yells. "Just because he dumped you, you want to get even." And suddenly they're all talking at once, making accusations, and I'm actually cringing, ready for physical blows, although I don't really think these girls would be violent. Their words are painful enough.

"You should just go back to wherever you came from," Emery says. "Go back to Loserville and leave us alone!"

Just then someone grabs my arm and jerks me, and bracing myself for a blow, I close my eyes in fear.

But when I open them, I see Zach's face. "Are you okay?" he asks with concern.

I just nod.

"Let's get you out of here." He escorts me away from the angry crowd.

I'm shaking so hard it's difficult to walk, but as we get farther away from their taunts and jeers, tears slide down my cheeks again.

"Do you want me to take you to the counseling center?"

"I . . . uh . . . I don't know." I feel slightly dizzy, like all I want is to get out of here, go home, hide in my bed.

But he just keeps walking and before long, I find myself back in Mrs. Evanston's office. She is just hanging up the phone and doesn't even look that surprised to see me. "Sit down." She points to the chair, then looks curiously at Zach.

"I'll go," he says as if he's uncomfortable.

"Thank you." She smiles at him.

Once again, she hands me some tissues, gives me a couple of minutes, then asks what happened. I quickly explain and she just nods. "I expected there'd be some backlash. But I'm surprised at Emery. She's usually more controlled than that."

"She's furious at me." I wipe my nose. "I think the whole school is."

"Not Zach Lowenstein. And he's a good guy to have on your side."

I nod.

"Well, I'll call Emery in for a little chat." She makes a note of something. "But I want to fill you in on what's going on with the DA's office first. I assume you haven't heard yet?"

"I haven't heard anything."

"The police arrested Harris this morning in the school parking lot. Unfortunately some of the students, including Emery, witnessed it."

"Oh." I try not to imagine Harris being handcuffed and placed in a patrol car.

"I just got off the phone with Detective Dorman. She said the DA decided to proceed with the case. Harris will remain in custody until he appears before the judge."

"When will that happen?"

"Probably today. And the judge will set his bail and an arraignment will be scheduled."

Suddenly the seriousness of this hits me. "So he'll be in jail?"

"Until his bail is paid. I assume his parents will pay it."

"Will he be back in school?"

"No, he's suspended indefinitely. Unless he is proven innocent."

"How long does all this take?"

"I'm not sure. But I'll try to keep you informed."

I think about the angry girls in the locker bay. "What am I going to do? I felt like they wanted to kill me out there."

"I'll try to run some damage control on the students. Emery is usually a reasonable girl, and she can exert her influence on the others."

"She might usually be reasonable, but she's enraged today."

"Do you feel unsafe?" She peers curiously at me.

I shrug. "I don't know . . . I was scared. I'm not used to being yelled at."

"Well, if you actually do feel unsafe, feel free to go to a security guard or come to the office. But I promise you, I will try to put a lid on it, even if I have to threaten more suspensions."

I take in a deep breath. How much angrier will everyone get if even more kids are suspended — *thanks to me?*

"One more thing, Haley."

"What?"

"Based on what you told us on Friday, Detective Dorman thinks it's possible Harris has done this to more girls than just you. Do you have any idea who the others, if there are others, might be?"

I shake my head. "Not at all."

"Perhaps you could ask around. If there were more girls, the case would be much stronger."

"I honestly don't know who I could ask—or who'd be willing to speak to me."

"Well, just keep your eyes and ears open. Sometimes when something like this comes out into the open, others become willing to speak out too. There's safety in numbers."

I nod. "Okay . . . I'll let you know if I learn anything."

"And remember, if you ever feel seriously threatened or unsafe, get help, Haley. I honestly don't think Emery and her friends will do anything beyond words, but you never know."

. . . .

For the rest of the day, Zach seems to be everywhere I am. At first I think it's a coincidence, but then when he meets me outside of economics before lunch, I get suspicious.

"Are you my new bodyguard?"

He chuckles. "Kind of. I asked Mrs. Evanston for a copy of your schedule so I could sort of help you through the day."

"Thanks," I quietly tell him. The truth is, I'm exceedingly grateful for this. And as he walks me into the cafeteria, where I'm getting looks from all directions, I feel even more appreciative. We get our food, then I go with him to a table where several kids are already seated. The only one I know among them is Poppie, but she and Zach do some quick introductions, although I'm afraid the names go in one ear and out the other.

I try to act natural with this group, and I am thankful for the welcome they give me, but it's like I can't really focus or think. More than ever I think Dad was right to set up a counseling session for me. I probably really do need some help.

When some of the kids try to direct questions concerning Harris toward me, Zach is quick to cut them off. "Just give her a break, guys. She's been through a lot already today."

In art I give Ms. Flores an update in the privacy of her office. "So you're doing okay?" she asks.

I shrug. "I've had better days."

She hugs me. "And you will again."

"Thanks. I hope so."

For the rest of the day, Zach plays bodyguard. When school is over, he offers to give me a ride home, which I gladly accept. As we walk out to the parking lot, I'm surprised that I never realized what a truly nice guy he is. Was I really that blind?

He opens the door to a small hybrid car and waits for me to get in. Feeling a little uncomfortable over this special attention, I hurry to get inside. Then as he goes around to the other side, I notice what looks like a church bulletin on the floor.

"How are you feeling?" He starts his car.

"I feel like I've just spent a day on the battlefield."

"It's going to get better."

"I want to believe that." I bend down and pick up the bulletin. "Is this yours?"

"Oh, yeah." He nods as he turns onto the street.

"My dad and I went to this church yesterday."

He tosses a surprised sideways glance at me. "You're kidding!"

"No. A friend of his goes there. And, well, after Dad heard about what I've been through, he thought maybe it was time for us to get back into church again. We used to go, back when my parents were still married, back before my mom went crazy."

"Your mom went crazy?"

"Well, not literally. Or maybe literally. I'm not sure, really. But about the same time my brother went to Iraq, my mom started going to this weird church, and she started acting different . . . and my parents split up. And I just quit church altogether."

"So where are you with your faith now?"

Feeling a little self-conscious, I explain about recommitting my life to God.

"Seriously?" His face lights up. "That is extremely cool, Haley. I'm really happy for you. Are you happy about it too?"

"It's kind of hard to imagine ever feeling *truly* happy again. But I do feel a little better . . . kind of like I have a bit of hope now. Before I was so bummed. . . . It was like I couldn't see any way out of this mess. Now I think maybe I can survive it after all. Even though . . . it's still really hard. Especially after today."

"I'll bet you that by the end of the week, kids won't even be talking about it anymore."

"I don't know about that. The end of the week is a football game, and if Mitchell loses because Harris is gone, I'm sure everyone will blame me."

"I suppose you could be right. But what you might not know is the JV team has a really good quarterback, Ben Stiles. He's only a sophomore, but I'm guessing they'll move him up to varsity now. I have a feeling he's even better than Harris. Plus, he's a really good guy. He goes to my church too."

"It seems like a nice church. We plan to go back next Sunday."

"What service did you go to?"

I tell him and he explains that if we went to the first service instead, I could attend the youth fellowship group afterward. "And if you like, I can drop you home. You know, if your dad wanted to leave after the worship service."

"That sounds good. Thanks." We're at the condo now. "I really appreciate you playing guardian angel for me, Zach." I reach for the door handle. "You have no idea."

"How about if I pick you up for school tomorrow? That might make it easier on you, in case you get mobbed again."

"You don't mind?"

He smiles. "Not at all."

I smile back. "You know, Zach, you're a lot better looking than John Lennon."

He throws back his head and laughs. "You just made my day, Haley."

I wave good-bye as I get out, and as I go up the stairs to our unit, I experience what almost feels like a tiny surge of happiness.

On the following day, with Zach still acting as my guardian angel, I feel a little more confident. And I even go as far as to take Libby aside in biology. The teacher is out and we're supposed to be doing lab work, but I feel like this is important. For some reason, I get the impression Libby's not part of Emery's we-hate-Haley club. "Are you as angry at me as Emery and the others?" I tentatively ask.

"No." She shakes her head. "Why should I be?"

"Do you mind if I ask you a question?"

She shrugs but looks a little uneasy.

I glance around to be sure no one is listening, and it looks safe. "Do you know the names of other girls who might've gone out with Harris, you know, during those brief breakup times? I remember you mentioned something about it before."

"Why are you asking me this?"

"Because there's a concern that I might not have been Harris's only victim," I say in a hushed tone.

Her eyes get bigger. "Oh."

I can tell she knows something. "Maybe we could talk during lunch. Would that be okay?"

"I don't know."

"Please," I beg. "At least hear me out. Okay?"

Her gaze darts around, as if she thinks someone might be watching.

"Please," I say again. "What he did was wrong, Libby, *illegal*. If he gets away with it . . . well, then we'll be to blame for any future victims."

"Okay," she says in a tight voice. "Meet me in the library, in the magazine section. Don't be late." Then she turns back to her lab and I go back to mine.

After biology I tell Zach about what I'm doing. "Do you think you could sort of watch to be sure no one else sees us? Libby is afraid to be seen talking to me."

"Sure," he agrees. "No problem."

I feel high expectations as Zach and I hurry to the library after fourth period, but when I get there, Libby is nowhere to be seen. "Do you think she chickened out?" Zach asks as we sit in the comfortable easy chairs to wait.

"I hope not."

Then just as we're ready to give up, Libby comes in through a back door. She motions to me from behind a bookshelf and I hurry to join her. "I probably shouldn't be doing this," she tells me.

"Yes, you should." Then I explain about the police's theory that I might not be an isolated case but how the lack of evidence is a concern. "If other girls have been hurt like me, their stories need to come out too. Otherwise, Harris could just keep doing this. Do you want him to get away with it?"

She shakes her head, then hands me a slip of paper. "I made a list."

"Thanks!"

"And I have no idea if those girls went through what you did. I suspect a lot of them knew exactly what they were getting into. But there's a couple—I put stars by their names—who might have a story to tell."

"This is great, Libby."

"I left one name off the list."

"One name?" I'm confused.

"Mine."

I try not to look shocked. *"Really?"*

"Last summer. I . . . well . . . I was the mystery girl Harris was with for a short while."

"So . . . did Harris, uh, did he hurt you?" I lower my voice. "I mean, did he rape you?"

She just nods and there are tears in her eyes.

"I'm sorry."

"I . . . well, I should've known better. I'd heard stories. But somehow I thought I'd be different. I thought he was really done with Emery. And I believed him when he said he loved me."

"I'm sad to say I know how you feel. Well, except I really didn't know better."

"I tried to warn you, Haley."

I frown. "You never said a word to me."

"I wrote you a note. Didn't you get it?"

A wave of regret rushes through me. "Yes, but it was anonymous . . . and I didn't believe it."

She shakes her head sadly. "I know I should've told you in person."

I sigh. "That might've made a difference. But that's exactly why we can't afford to remain silent now, Libby. Other girls need to be protected and it's up to us to blow the lid off this thing."

She still looks uneasy. "Well, you have the list."

I thank her and tuck the list into my jeans pocket, then we go our separate ways. Zach is still waiting for me and I give him a thumbs-up. We hurry to the cafeteria, where we both grab a quick lunch and I explain that I want to take the list to Mrs. Evanston. "She can get it to the police," I tell him as we walk toward the office. We just catch her returning from her own lunch and she invites us into her office.

"Here's a list of names." I hand her the paper. "I don't even know who most of these girls are, and some might not have been actual victims, but some probably were. And there's one name not on the list." Now I tell her about Libby.

Mrs. Evanston shakes her head, and her eyes grow wide when she reads the list. "This is so wrong . . . so sad . . . on so many levels."

"So you'll see that the police or the DA or whatever gets it?"

"Of course, but I'd like to do more than just that." She looks hopefully at me. "It would help if I had your cooperation."

"My cooperation?" I feel worried now. All I want is for all this to be over and to get a life back with some semblance of normality.

"I'd like to invite a special counselor in. Someone who knows how to help victims of rape. I'd like to set up some group therapy for the girls who suffered."

"Why do you need my cooperation?"

"I'd like you to help lead the group."

"Me?" I blink. "Lead a group of rape victims? I don't think so."

"I know it probably sounds overwhelming right now, but maybe you could give it some time . . . just think about it."

"I'll think about it, and I might even attend a group like that. But leading it . . . well, I just can't imagine doing that."

She thanks me for the list, and Zach and I hurry off to art, where we are all busily getting things ready for Thursday night's fall art fair. It feels good to be busy like this. I love that Ms. Flores is comfortable asking me to do things to help—the kinds of things I'm comfortable doing, not leading a group of rape victims!

. . . .

During the next couple of days, rumors circulate regarding Harris. Mostly I try to ignore them, but it's impossible not to hear some things. Finally I decide that perhaps it's better not to be like an ostrich with my head buried, and I ask Zach if he can bring me up to date.

Apparently he's been paying attention, because according to him, Harris is currently (1) out on bail, (2) claiming he's innocent, (3) hiring an expensive attorney, and (4) planning a countersuit against me for defamation of character and other things. I don't even know how to respond to this news. But Zach hugs me and assures me that it will be okay. However, I have my doubts. Lots and lots of doubts.

As Dad drives me to the art fair, I tell him the latest news.

"Don't let Harris get to you. I'm sure he's just trying to intimidate you. He's obviously used to getting his way. But I'm sure no judge will be interested in hearing a countersuit in a case like this."

"Well, it's still pretty intimidating," I confess.

"Even so, you need to stick to your guns, Haley. The truth will eventually come out. I'm sure of it. Just be strong, sweetie. In due time, this will all be behind you."

I wish I felt as confident as Dad. As we go into the school, where lots of parents are visiting tonight, what little self-assurance I had built up in regard to the art fair is quickly unraveling.

"Hold your head high." Dad pats me on the back. "You know who you are and it doesn't matter what others say or think."

"Right." I try to make a brave smile, then leave him at our improvised "coffeehouse" while I go to find my pottery station. Since I knew I was doing something messy, throwing pots, I dressed pretty casually tonight. Just jeans and a plaid flannel shirt, plus I put my hair in two braids. At the time it made sense, but now that I'm seeing a lot of the students dressed up and stylish, I'm not so sure. Just the same, I take my place at the potting wheel and, focusing on my work, I get started.

Zach waves to me from the table where he's doing block printing, as does Poppie from where she's sitting in front of an easel, working on a canvas. Before long a group of grade school kids come over and start to watch me. I casually tell them what I'm doing, field some of their questions, and am just starting to feel good about this whole thing when I sense someone staring at me.

I pause, wiping my hands on the rag in my lap, and look up to see a middle-aged couple scowling at me. I have no idea how I know this, but I am absolutely certain that these tall and relatively attractive people are Harris's parents.

I lock eyes with the woman for a moment, but there is so much pure hatred in her expression that I'm forced to turn away. Seriously, if looks could kill, I'd be a goner. As it is, my hands start to shake and I'm worried that I'm going to blow this pot, which I'd hoped to transform into a bowl.

I dip my hands in water. *God, please, please, please help me through this uncomfortable moment.* It's not the first time I've prayed lately, but it might be the most desperate time. My hands are trembling.

"Why are you getting your hands wet?" a boy with dark curly hair asks me.

"That helps to smooth out the pot." I carefully hold my hands on the clay. "See how much smoother it's getting?"

"Can I try it?" he asks.

I'm tempted to say no, worried that he'll mess it up. But I could just as easily mess it up if my hands don't stop shaking. "Sure. Come over here and dip your hands in the water, and I'll let you give it a try. You have to be gentle though."

With wide eyes he comes over and I instruct him on what to do. "That feels cool," he says as his hands cup the pot. "It's so *smooth*."

"That's because of the water."

Just then he presses too hard and the whole thing goes lopsided and flops over. He jumps back, holding his hands in the air. "I'm sorry! I didn't mean to do that."

"It's okay."

"But I ruined it," he says sadly. "I'm really sorry."

"Really, it's okay. Clay is totally reusable and very forgiving. If you ruin a pot during this stage, it's no big deal." I glance over to see Harris's parents still standing there, looking like they want to kill me. "It's after the pottery has been fired in the kiln that it hurts to mess with it."

I point to my finished pots displayed nearby. "Now, if you dropped and broke one of those, I might not be too happy. That damage would be permanent and unfixable." I throw the lump of clay into the slop bucket and smile at the boy. "But at this stage, I'll just start over." As I wedge a fresh piece of clay, I explain the process of removing the air bubbles and why this is so important.

"You mean it'd really explode in the kiln," the curly haired boy asks, "like a *bomb*?"

I nod as I slam the ball of clay onto the wheel—bull's-eye. "Yes, and the exploding pot wouldn't be the only one ruined. It would probably damage all the other pottery sitting around it." I glance back up at the woman. "Kind of like when someone does something bad, like breaking the law, and everyone around him ends up suffering because of it. It's not fair, but that's just how it goes."

The woman blinks in surprise. But the next time I look up, the couple has moved past my station. Meanwhile the kids stay on, talking about everything from exploding bombs to the case of a neighbor's stolen dog. I am grateful for their friendly company.

Toward the end of the event, Ms. Flores and Dad come over. "I told your dad I'd let you take a break," she says to me. "So you can show him around a little. Sound good?"

I nod and wipe my hands on a rag. "My shoulders are starting to ache." As I clean up, Dad and Ms. Flores chat congenially, almost like they're old friends, and I realize how nice it is to see Dad with a woman who's not only intelligent and good but also closer to his age. Not that I'm playing matchmaker, but it is reassuring.

I show Dad around and even introduce him to some of my friends like Zach and Poppie. Then as we're getting a snack at the "coffeehouse," I tell him about the couple I suspect was Harris's parents and how they gave me the icy treatment.

"Are they still here?" Dad glances around as if he'd like to have a word with them.

"I don't see them now."

"Probably a good thing."

All in all, the fall art fair turned out to be surprisingly fun. Despite the moment of discomfort with Harris's parents, I enjoyed myself. And by the time Dad and I are driving home, I feel stronger. Maybe this battle will be won by baby steps—one at a time.

However, I'm learning that recovering from rape is a slow and unpredictable process. Later on, awakened in the middle of the night, I'm so shaken and frightened that hot tears stream down my cheeks and I feel sick to my stomach. I barely remember details of the nightmare—just the very real sensations of suffocation, pure fear, and complete desperation. But I know it was about the rape . . . and all I can do is pray, begging God to hold me in his arms and comfort me.

. . . .

Zach turns out to be right about a couple of things. For one, Ben Stiles does turn out be a fantastic quarterback. He joins the varsity team and continues leading them through a nearly perfect season and then on to state, where Mitchell takes third place. Already there is talk of college scholarship possibilities for Ben, and no one disputes the fact that he has far more athletic potential than Harris.

The other thing Zach was mostly right about is that everyone at school really has seemed to move on. Other than Emery and a few of her closest friends, no one is treating me much like poison now. Not that I have any desire to be around those kids anymore. I have my own circle of friends now—a combination of art and music kids—and a place where I can be myself.

Mrs. Evanston, true to her word, did locate a counselor from the women's crisis center, and so far she's helped with three group counseling sessions where I actually stepped up to the task and acted as the leader. Fortunately, Bonnie (the counselor) handles the tough stuff. I just organize things, make sure the girls know about it, and get snacks brought in. The first meeting only has three girls, including me, but to my surprise it's a girl who wasn't even raped by Harris who opens up.

"It was a neighbor boy who raped me," Elise tells us with lowered eyes. "I was only thirteen when it happened. He was in high school and I couldn't believe he was being so nice to me. And even though my mom told me not to spend time with him, I honestly believed he really liked me. I know now that it was dumb. He was just grooming me, telling me what he knew I wanted to hear . . . so he could get what he wanted."

She takes in a deep breath. "He asked me to show him the playhouse in our backyard, and I stupidly took him out there." She shudders. "And you know what happened after that."

"Did you tell?" I ask her. "Was he arrested?"

She shakes her head no.

"You have to tell," I urge her. "You can't let him get away with that, Elise."

She looks up with tearful brown eyes. "But it's been more than two years."

"That doesn't matter," Bonnie tells her. "You still need to report it. You might be able to prevent someone else's victimization."

"What happened after you were raped?" the other girl asks. "I mean, did it ever happen again?'"

"No way!" Elise's eyes darken. "I would never let him . . . even if he wanted to. I hate him."

Bonnie takes over, explaining the steps Elise needs to take. And she talks about the stages of grief that happen after an experience like that. Something about Elise's vulnerability as she told her story helps us to chime in too, and by the end of the first session, Elise actually seems encouraged. We all hug and promise to come back next week.

Thanks to word-of-mouth "advertising," our numbers double in our second meeting. And by our third meeting ten girls are present. The purpose of the meetings is to give girls a forum to talk and learn and form a kind of solidarity. And I'm surprised at how airing our stories makes everyone feel better. It's like a load gets lifted from our shoulders.

Elise takes Bonnie's advice by filing a police report. It takes about a month before a small group of girls complete police reports regarding Harris. According to the district attorney, the case against Harris is getting stronger all the time and, if all goes well, his trial is expected to be scheduled for after the new year.

I try not to think about that because I have to testify and I'm still not sure how I'm going to handle that. But having our group therapy sessions is making me stronger every time. And knowing that I won't be the only one testifying is hugely reassuring. There truly is comfort in numbers.

Still, if I could just bury the whole thing without anyone else getting hurt and pretend that none of this ever happened to me, I gladly would. It's not easy surviving something like that. Fortunately, I don't think about it all the time. Sometimes I go a whole day without thinking about it. Then, sometimes, just when I think I'm doing better, I experience another horrible dream. I wake up sweating and shaking and frightened, and I am reminded—like a slap in the face—that it was real. All too real.

Occasionally something happens at school where I suddenly feel self-conscious and insecure and just plain negative about myself—as if I really am damaged beyond repair. But then I try to remember that God is able to fix me. At least that's what I'm trying to believe. Sometimes it seems too good to be true.

As it gets closer to Christmas, I am feeling much stronger, and I ask Dad if we can invite my brother to join us for the holidays.

"I'd love to have Sean come down here," he tells me. "But Sean hasn't been speaking to me."

"What if I call him and ask?" I suggest.

"Great. And if you can talk him into coming, I'll pay for his plane ticket."

So after school I make the call. Naturally, my mom is the one who answers. As usual, she sounds grumpy . . . and pious. "My ladies' group has been praying for you. They're all very worried about your spiritual well-being, Haley. You and your father are in a dangerous place."

For a moment I consider really shocking her by telling her about the rape, but it would probably just blow up in my face. Instead I tell her about how Dad and I are going to church now. "We really like it," I say cheerfully. "It's kind of like our old church, only bigger. And the youth group is really great. I've made some good friends."

"Oh." There is a long silence and I think maybe I've given her something to think about.

"Anyway, I wanted to talk to Sean. Is he around?"

"Of course he's around. Where else would he be? All he does is watch violent movies and play video games."

I want to question why she allows that in her house but don't want to rock Sean's unstable world too much. After a long wait, Sean comes to the phone. "Hey, Hay," he says in a depressed tone.

"Hey, Sean. I miss you, bro!"

"Miss you too." Still flat, depressed, broken.

"I'm really enjoying being down here with Dad. He's really changed, Sean. In good ways, I mean. And we'd love it if you could come down and visit for a while during Christmas. Do you want to?"

"I don't know."

"You know Mom doesn't really celebrate Christmas anymore," I remind him. "So it's not like you'll be missing anything. And our church is going to have a cool service, and the music is really good."

"I don't know . . ." he says again.

"Please, Sean. Will you do it for me? I'd love to have at least part of our family together. And Dad will pay for your plane ticket."

"A plane ticket?" For some reason this seems to pique his interest—like he knows Dad is serious about wanting him to visit.

"Yeah. And we'll plan some fun things to do while you're here. I don't think you'll be sorry."

"Well, I guess I could go down there, just for a few days anyway."

"Great!" Now we go over when he should fly down and how long he should stay, and I promise to get back to him. "I can't wait to see you, Sean!"

"Yeah . . ." Flat voice again. "Me, too."

By the end of the day, Dad's booked Sean a flight and I e-mail the information to him. Then I spend a couple afternoons cleaning the condo, getting it ready for Sean. I even put up Christmas decorations, and Dad and I get a tree and do some Christmas shopping.

"I want this to be Sean's best Christmas since getting home from Iraq," I tell Dad. "It's like he's missed out on so much. Maybe it will make a difference to him."

Dad smiles sadly. "Just don't get your hopes up too high."

"I won't. Mostly I'll just be glad to see him. Poor guy, he deserves a break from Mom."

"I wish your mom could get a break too." Dad shakes his head. "From herself anyway."

. . . .

Sean arrives two days before Christmas, and he actually seems a tiny bit more like his old self as he tells us about the turbulence on the flight. Maybe the flight shook something into him. To celebrate Sean's homecoming, Dad takes us out to dinner. I try not to cringe when I realize he's taking us to the same steakhouse where Harris took me—back in another lifetime. But Sean seems to appreciate it and orders a humongous steak, which he easily consumes.

"Looks like you've been building up an appetite," Dad tells him.

Sean shrugs. "Mom doesn't cook much anymore."

There's a long silence and I know we're all thinking pretty much the same thing, but what can we say?

"Tonight we're going to watch *It's a Wonderful Life*," I say just to get the conversation going again. "Remember how we used to love it?"

Sean shrugs again. "I guess."

It's pretty quiet on the way back, and I'm thankful we have an activity to do together tonight. When we get home, I make microwave popcorn and put out the plate of brownies I made yesterday, and to my relief, Sean seems almost happy to be with us — and to be here.

As we watch the movie, he loosens up some, and I can tell by his expression that he's really getting into it. And when the scene comes up where George Bailey is about to jump off the bridge, Sean starts crying.

Dad grabs the remote and turns off the TV and we both turn to Sean. "Do you need to talk, son?" Dad asks softly.

Sean just shakes his head. "No one would understand."

I've heard him say this same thing before . . . many times. But this time, I decide to challenge him and I actually stand up. "You know what? You might be surprised at what I would understand."

Dad nods, leaning back as if to give me the floor.

"Really?" Sean's tone is skeptical. "In your sixteen and a half years, living as a protected princess, you think you can relate to what I've been through?"

"Not completely, Sean. But you might be surprised to hear that I'm being treated for PTSD."

He does look surprised. "What for? Did you get a bad grade in algebra?"

I take in a deep breath, then begin telling him about being raped. I don't go into all the details but share just enough to get his attention.

"I'm sorry, Haley. I had no idea."

"Mom doesn't know. But I thought maybe you needed to hear about it."

"And you're really getting PTSD counseling?"

"I've been going for about six weeks, and I think I'm ready to move on now."

"Did it do you any good?"

I nod eagerly. "Yes. The counselor knows her stuff. She's very helpful. She gives you tools to deal with things."

"Maybe you'd like to meet her," Dad suggests.

Sean shrugs. "I don't know."

"What could it hurt?" I ask.

Sean looks at Dad and then at me and nods. "Yeah, I guess it couldn't."

"And if you discover that the counseling helps," Dad tells him, "you'd be welcome to stick around here and continue with it. Maybe you could look into the local community college. I hear it's a good one."

Sean sighs. "I do have GI money for that."

"You used to like school," I say.

He just nods, then points to the TV. "Can we finish the movie now?"

So Dad turns it back on and we sit there together, watching the story of a good man whose life appears to fall completely apart and how, with the help and love of friends and family, he gets it back together. Appropriate, I think.

· · · · · · · · · ·

Harris's trial is scheduled for the second week of January, and as the day draws closer, I get increasingly nervous. Despite Dad and Sean and my friends at school encouraging me that it'll be okay, I am feeling pretty scared. But then so are the other girls who will be testifying at his trial. As a result, Bonnie holds a special meeting to let us practice for court. We take turns sitting in the witness stand, a chair in front, and Bonnie plays the defense by questioning us. Some of her questions are hard and hurtful. And sometimes we cry.

"I'm sorry to do this," Bonnie tells us after our first session. "But it's very possible you'll be treated like that in the court-room, and I just want you to remain strong and to tell the truth." By the end of the second session, just a few days before the trial, we all feel like we can do this.

Both Dad and Sean go with me to the trial. I'm surprised at how Sean really seems to be changing, not back to his old self but into a stronger person. Right now, sitting across the room from Harris, I need all the strength I can get. Dressed in a sharp-looking navy suit, he holds his handsome head up, like he's here to prove his innocence. I notice the same middle-aged couple from the art show sitting directly behind Harris. It seems I had them pegged.

I glance at Dad and Sean and feel a rush of relief just know-ing my family is here for me. It's also encouraging knowing that Zach is sitting right behind us. Plus a number of the other girls are here with their families for support.

However, I discover there's a lot to get aggravated about in court. Everything seems to take forever, and you can't shout out when someone tells a lie. And hearing Harris painting these totally bogus scenes and acting like he's the victim makes me want to scream. But I control myself, remembering that I'll get my chance. At least I hope I will. Because all the victims have written their statements and the DA has presented them as evidence to the judge, we don't all have to take the witness stand. So it's possible I won't even be asked to go up. But eventually I do get my turn, and it's weird because I'm almost eager.

But after I take an oath to tell the truth, it's unnerving to see Harris sitting just a few feet away from me. I stare at him for a moment, and for some reason he doesn't look like how I remembered him. I'm not sure if he's changed or if I have, but instead of being gorgeous like I thought he was before, he seems flat and ordinary to me. Almost like a cardboard cutout.

Bonnie's mock-trial training turns out to be fairly accurate, so I'm not too shocked by the insinuations and outright lies coming from the defense.

"Is it true that you *invited* Harris into your home on the night of the *alleged* rape?" the attorney asks. She is middle-aged and slightly motherly looking, but there's a meanness in her eyes.

"Yes."

"And is it true that this wasn't the first time Harris had been in your home?"

"Yes."

"And is it true that you invited Harris into your home with the full knowledge that your father was not at home."

"No . . ." I try to remember. "I wasn't totally sure that—"

"You have sworn to tell the truth, Miss McLean."

"I *am* telling the truth. I wasn't sure if my dad was home or not."

"Yes, but you were aware that your father was out on a *date*." She says the word as if it's something immoral.

"Yes, but I thought he might be home."

"And on the night you invited Harris to take a late-night swim with you, is it true that your father was out with his girlfriend then?"

"I did *not* invite Harris for a late-night swim," I tell her. "That was his idea."

"Whose pool did you use?"

"It's the condo pool."

"So you were playing hostess," she states. "You let Harris change his clothes in your house while your father was out. You allowed him to swim in your pool. Or did he force his way?"

"Harris *asked* to go swimming. I did not invite him."

"But you agreed?"

"Yes."

Her line of questioning goes on for a while and I try to give honest answers, but she often cuts me off when it suits her. Eventually I get so frustrated that a few tears slip out and I'm worried I'll botch the whole trial. Eventually the DA gets his turn and I am allowed to tell what really happened that horrible night. And after what feels like hours, the judge finally excuses me.

As I leave the witness stand, I'm shaking so badly I'm not sure I can walk in a straight line back to my seat. As I pass by where Harris is sitting, I catch him sneering at me and I can't help but stare back. However, I say nothing, just continue to my seat, where Dad and Sean both smile and squeeze my hands and tell me I did great. Zach pats me on the back. And I try to just breathe.

However, I'm so numb that a lot of the rest of the trial washes over me. Then finally the judge bangs his gavel, and I think he's about to declare Harris guilty or not guilty. Instead, he says the court will take a recess while the jury deliberates.

Dad and Sean manage to eat lunch, but my stomach is in tight little knots. All I can think is, what if our evidence isn't sufficient to convict him? What if Harris walks away? What if he launches a countersuit against me? Still, I don't voice these doubts.

God, please help the jurors to make the right decision.

Then, suddenly, it's time to go back into court, and the room is filled with anticipation as we all return to our seats, waiting for the verdict. I grab both Dad's and Sean's hands, holding tightly to them while we wait. I try to listen as one of the jury members says something, but my brain is too fuzzy and I feel slightly dizzy and almost sick. But then Dad and Sean and all the others on our side are beginning to cheer and clap.

It's over. Harris has been convicted. He has been declared GUILTY!

But here is the weirdest part of this very weird day. I look over and see his parents sobbing and holding on to each other, and then Harris turns around and, seeing them, he breaks into tears too, and I feel no sense of victory. In fact, I have tears running down my cheeks too. And all I can think is, what a waste. What a sad and crazy and unfortunate waste.

I'm so upset that I have to turn away. But Dad and Sean and Zach all hug me, and we leave that sad, dark place and go out to where the sun is shining way too brightly. I feel raw and weak . . . almost as if the skin has been peeled off me.

"You did great," Zach tells me. Then he hugs me again and promises to call, and I am left with Dad and Sean. But I still feel strange, like none of this was real, like it can't truly be over — not just like that. Surely someone is going to pull the rug out from under me again.

"You saw it through," Dad tells me as we walk to the car. "I'm proud of you."

"Me, too." Sean slaps me on the back, jolting me back into the here and now, making me believe that maybe this really is over. "Way to go, sis. Now that jerk will end up right where he belongs."

"Will he really have to serve *twelve years?*" I ask Dad. For some reason, twelve years sounds like forever. Not that I want Harris to get off easy. I just don't want to feel guilty about his sentencing. I want to be free of all parts of this.

Dad shrugs. "I don't know if too many people serve their full sentences these days. And there's always the chance his attorney will appeal, although I don't see the point."

"Well, I'm glad it's over," I admit. "But I guess I feel sorry for Harris's family." I don't mention that I actually feel a tiny bit sorry for Harris as well. I don't think they'd understand that. Just the same, when I think of what he did to me and the other girls, I'm not sorry. And I'm very relieved that he will be unable to hurt anyone else.

As we drive home, I realize that I need to forgive Harris. It's something I've been thinking about off and on for weeks. But I've never been able to really take it head-on. Not until now. Suddenly I remember something the youth pastor said a couple of weeks ago.

"Refusing to forgive someone is like drinking poison and then assuming the other person is going to die. The truth is, you are simply killing yourself."

I run those words around in my head as we drive home. If I don't forgive Harris, I am hurting myself. I need to let go of this horrible offense. Not so much for Harris as for myself. And somehow that makes it a little easier.

I close my eyes and silently pray. *God, I choose to forgive Harris for raping me. I want to put this painful memory to rest and move on.*

As simple as that sounds, it feels like it worked, and I believe God is helping me. Although I suspect I may have to go through these steps again. I remember the Bible verse about forgiving seventy times seven. At that rate, it might take nearly five hundred more times for me to completely forgive Harris.

But as Dad parks the car at the condo, I realize that right now, at this very moment, it feels like I've really forgiven him. It's like a weight has been lifted from me, and I realize that God must've been the one doing the lifting, and it's a huge relief. I don't want to keep drinking poison.

Once we're in the condo, I decide that I will write Harris a letter and send it to the prison. Not today, but someday I will write him a letter and tell him that I forgive him. And I'll make it clear that my forgiveness isn't a way of saying that I don't think he was wrong, wrong, wrong in what he did to me and the other girls. I will simply state that I am forgiving him because God has forgiven me and because I don't want to be poisoned by my own unforgiveness.

I might even tell him about what I've been learning lately. According to what our pastor says and from what I've been reading in the Bible, I have become convinced that God thoroughly enjoys fixing and saving things that are broken. That means no matter how hurt and defeated you feel, no matter how badly you have been damaged, God can repair you. God can give anyone a second chance. Even someone like Harris Stephens.

1. Early in the story, you can see that Haley has some challenges, but for the most part, she seems like a fairly grounded character. What part of her personality do you most relate to and why?

2. What three words would you use to describe Haley's mother? Explain why.

3. What three words would you use to describe Haley's father? Explain why.

4. On a scale of one to ten (one = feeling imprisoned and ten = having complete freedom), what number would you say Haley experienced with her mother? And later with her father? What number would best describe your own home?

5. What was your first impression of Harris Stephens? How would you respond to a guy who came across like that in a relationship with you? Be honest.

6. What were your first impressions of Zack and Poppie, Haley's art class acquaintances?

7. What did you think the first time Harris came into Haley's condo when her father was gone? If you were Haley's best friend, what would you have said about that?

8. How did you respond to the scene where Harris raped Haley? Describe how it made you feel.

9. What could Haley have done (if anything) to have prevented being raped?

10. How do you think date rape compares to rape? Why do you think it's so underreported? How would you help a friend who was in a similar situation?

11. Why do you think Haley had such a hard time telling anyone about what happened to her? How could she have handled it differently?

12. What was the most important thing you learned from reading this book?

MELODY CARLSON has written more than three hundred books for all age groups, but she particularly enjoys writing for teens. Perhaps this is because her own teen years remain so vivid in her memory. After claiming to be an atheist at the ripe old age of twelve, she later surrendered her heart to Jesus and has been following him ever since. Her hope and prayer for all her readers is that each one would be touched by God in a special way through her stories. For more information, please visit Melody's website at www.melodycarlson.com.

Lonely? Jealous? Hurt?
Melody Carlson addresses the
issues you face today.

The TRUECOLORS Series

The TRUECOLORS series addresses issues that most affect teen girls. By taking on these difficult topics without being phony or preachy, best-selling author Melody Carlson challenges you to stay true to who you are and what you believe.

Dark Blue
(Loneliness)
9781576835296

Faded Denim
(Eating Disorders)
9781576835371

Deep Green
(Jealousy)
9781576835302

Bright Purple
(Homosexuality)
9781576839508

Torch Red
(Sex)
9781576835319

Moon White
(Witchcraft)
9781576839515

Pitch Black
(Suicide)
9781576835326

Harsh Pink
(Popularity)
9781576839522

Burnt Orange
(Drinking)
9781576835333

9781576835296

Fool's Gold
(Materialism)
9781576835340

Blade Silver
(Cutting)
9781576835357

Bitter Rose
(Divorce)
9781576835364

9781576835319

9781576835302

9781576835364

To order copies, call NavPress at
1-800-366-7788 or log on to
www.NavPress.com.

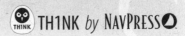